Manuel and the Lady

PEDRO C. LÓPEZ

iUniverse, Inc.
Bloomington

Manuel and the Lady

iUniverse books may be ordered through booksellers or by contacting:

iUniverse
1663 Liberty Drive
Bloomington, IN 47403
www.iuniverse.com
1-800-Authors (1-800-288-4677)

ISBN: 978-1-4620-4514-3 (sc)
ISBN: 978-1-4620-4516-7 (e)
ISBN: 978-1-4620-4515-0 (dj)

Library of Congress Control Number: 2011914243

Printed in the United States of America

iUniverse rev. date: 9/9/2011

To Lady, who loves the rain.

Chapter I

The first glimpse of the apartment building appalled Manuel. The structure, at least on the outside, looked beat-up and dilapidated, almost as if a small tornado or a minor earthquake had hit it. Many of the wall shingles, of a sickly green color, hung loosely and askew; some had fallen off altogether, leaving empty black patches where the tarpaper showed.

"Don't be fooled by the building's appearance," Juan said cheerily, perhaps reading his half-brother's mind. He had a round chubby face with pink cheeks and very thin lips. His lips were so thin that they looked like a mere slit. Despite being only in his twenties, he was beginning to show thinning hair on the crown of his head. "The inside of our apartment is really quite nice."

Next to the apartment building to its right, there was a little yard surrounded by a five-foot wire fence. Manuel had gotten a glimpse of the yard, which seemed to mirror the unpleasant outward aspect of the building. The yard looked water-starved; only here and there sprouted tufts of withered grass. Furthermore, it had been overrun with rocks, sticks, discarded car tires, and disfigured toys. Garbage spilled partially from huge corroded black trash tanks.

When Manuel entered the apartment's gloomy passageway, a hellish pungent stench immediately gripped his nostrils. There was almost as much disorder inside as outside. Furthermore, the hallway contained so much junk it gave the impression the tenants had come to consider it a sort of public storage facility. Suddenly, Manuel felt so repelled by the unsavory smells and crude sights that he regretted for a moment having left a beautiful, sunny, warm, and well-kept Miami to move to this seemingly ugly, sordid, grey, chilly Lawrence in the state of Massachusetts. Obviously, Lawrence wasn't a tourist town like Miami and thus didn't have to stay spruced up and neat and sparkling all the time. The Miami apartment building he had lived in, while unpretentious, had definitely lacked the repellent, squalid qualities prevalent inside and around this one.

Pablo and Juan carried the Cruzes' four bulging suitcases up the creaking narrow staircase, one suitcase per hand. Several boxes full of Maria's household paraphernalia still remained in the luggage compartment of Juan and Pablo's car, a two-door Ford Fairlane sedan painted in two colors, black on the top two-thirds and white on the lower third. Manuel, however, had decided to carry, on his first climb up the infernal-looking place, only his well-worn copy of the *Divine Comedy*. It was one of his most treasured possessions, a memento, a gift from the Stricklands, the family that had taken him in as one of their own at their home in Winnetka, Illinois, a month after he had arrived, unaccompanied by any member of his real family, in the United States as part of the U.S. Government-sponsored Operation Peter Pan. On the

Miami-Boston flight, he had taken the book with him and read from it, slowly and carefully, during most of the trip. Thanks to the Stricklands, especially Mrs. Strickland, he had acquired the habit of reading literature books from the great writers of the past.

As he reached the top landing, he heard sounds of instrumental music floating up to the third floor. From out of the gentle waves of wind and stringed instruments, a female voice rose and broke into a melancholic song. Suddenly, the soft gush of deep lament exploded into a thunderclap of shrill distortion.

"Maria Callas," Juan smiled, "from *Madame Butterfly.*"

"The old Italian lady downstairs is off her rocker again," Pablo added critically, and shook his head while making a face. "When she's having a nervous breakdown, she turns on her record-player full blast and shakes up the whole world with her operas."

After they had entered Pablo and Juan's apartment, Maria suddenly ordered: "Manuel, do something. Don't just stand there holding a book!"

"Oh, we'll take care of everything, Maria," Juan said, grinning at Maria with his thin lips and perfect white teeth.

By "we" he meant himself and Pablo, Manuel intuited.

"Please relax, Maria," Pablo intervened. "Let us first show you our little apartment."

Manuel watched his mother smile back at her stepson's friend Pablo, who appeared to be about the same age as his half-brother. Manuel felt very glad that Pablo was much younger than Maria. It guaranteed a certain tranquility of mind for Manuel. Even more comforting was the fact that Pablo was no James Dean in terms of looks. Pablo was short and bowed-legged and had intensely wavy black hair and olive skin as well as a muscular frame and flat nose that did him no favor but instead gave him the appearance of a rough-looking pugilist with a losing record. Manuel's mother, on the other hand, was a beautiful tall woman with hazel eyes and very white skin. She had thick copious brown hair, a fine straight nose, and sensuous fleshy lips—features Manuel had inherited from her. When people saw his mother and him together, they often remarked about how much they looked alike.

"See what I told you about not minding the exterior," Juan remarked enthusiastically. "What a difference between what you saw outside and what you see in here, huh? We wallpapered the whole apartment and bought new furniture last month. It's our way of making your arrival more pleasant! We wanted to make sure you'd feel at home right away. Now isn't all this just nice and beautiful? Small *but nice and beautiful.* Our own cozy little nest!" he chirped, and threw an arm over his half-brother Esteban's shoulders.

Juan's words pleased Manuel. In fact, they seemed to touch a deep emotional chord inside the younger brother.

In Cuba, Manuel had somehow developed the idea that Juan resented him for his looking up to his father like some sort of idol or hero. Of course, it was true that he had always held, as far back as he could remember, a special place in his heart for his dad. Manuel had always been seized with an overwhelming sense of joy every time Manolo had returned home from one of his frequent long trips to other parts of the island or abroad, bringing Manuel and his younger son Esteban all kinds of presents along with warm hugs and kisses, kisses that tickled Manuel's cheek with his trim, spiky black moustache. On such occasions the mere sight of his dad made Manuel feel as if the very sun had just strutted in through the front door of their house in Caibarien, Las Villas.

Still Manuel had never been able to fathom a logical reason for Juan's show of resentment toward him just on account of his admiration for the father he and Juan shared. Often he would be struck with the suspicion that such feelings on the part of his half-brother rode on top of those of jealousy, jealousy over the thought that Manuel might be Manolo's favorite son or something along that line. With less frequency he would be invaded with the idea that Juan hated his father Manolo because Manolo was a philandering man and Juan disliked the thought that his father's sins might be passed down to one of the sons.

But now here in the United States, Manuel thought, the chemistry appeared to have begun to change for the better between the two half-brothers. Lawrence, Massachusetts, seemed to have made Juan more affable and fraternal.

"The apartment is not big but it'll be just perfect for the five of us," Juan presently said, and began conducting the tour of the place.

He showed the Cruzes the kitchen and dining room first. The dining table was impressively modern; it had a shiny glass top and thick metallic cylindrically-shaped column legs. He pointed out that the frames of the table and the chairs were made of brass.

"When we purchased the dining set, we made sure

it was big enough to sit the whole family comfortably," Juan explained.

Manuel liked the sound of the word "family" and smiled at Juan.

"Yeah, that's exactly the reason we chose this set with six chairs," Pablo broke in. "Sufficient to have even a guest over for dinner. Who knows? Maybe Manolo will show up one of these days," he said, and winked at Maria.

"He can stay put in Miami with his whore," she quickly snapped, "for all I care.

Juan raised his eyebrows at her and tilted his head in the direction of Esteban. Manuel looked at Esteban and saw embarrassment and confusion in his younger brother's face. He had always felt very protective of Esteban, who, unfortunately, had not been awarded by nature the physical attributes he enjoyed. Just like his father Manolo, Esteban had a bony frame with thin legs. He was a candidate for future crooked adult teeth, unless some dental miracle was performed on him in the near future. His skin color was Mediterranean, just as his dad's. Furthermore, unlike Manuel, he had never distinguished himself in school, either academically or athletically. While it was generally said that Manuel looked like Maria, it was often commented that Esteban was the spitting image of Manolo.

"I was only teasing," Pablo apologized, and continued the tour of the apartment by passing on to one of the bedrooms, his and Juan's. The bedroom furniture there was brand-new and looked modern and stylish. It fit rather snugly inside the room. The platform bed was a queen size with an upholstered headboard.

"Top-grain leather," Pablo commented proudly, caressing the edge of the headboard with a hand.

"The whole set is made of teak wood," Juan added.

"Are they yours?" Manuel asked him, pointing at a couple of framed paintings hanging on one of the bedroom walls.

"Yes."

"Cardinals?"

"Right," Juan beamed.

Each painting looked like a close replica of the other. Both showed a nest full of baby birds, their bills anxiously wide-open, about to be fed by an adult bird.

"See the binoculars on the dresser?" Pablo said. "They're part of his new hobby: bird-watching. But the birds he likes to watch are not only of the feathered type but of the non-feathered one, too," he grinned. "In the summer those field binoculars of his are his constant companion on a lake in New Hampshire, and I swear he could tell you the migratory pattern and the mating call of every bikini-clad chick that passes in front of him."

Manuel and his younger brother Esteban looked at each other and shook with laughter.

The other bedroom where Maria and Esteban would sleep contained a bedroom set with two twin beds, a dresser with a mirror, and two night stands. Although a bit plain-looking, the set had obviously also been recently purchased and smelled fresh.

A wooden crucifix had been affixed to a wall above and between the two beds.

Manuel was told he would sleep in the comfortable leather convertible sofa in the parlor. Pablo removed the sofa cushions and pulled out the bed part to show him how spacious and comfortable a bed the sofa quickly turned into. Manuel nodded happily in agreement, his nostrils full of the strong smell of new leather.

After the Cruzes were shown the bathroom, Juan announced he and Pablo would finish carting up the rest of the Cruzes' belongings from the car. While involved in the small tour of the house, everyone had seemed to become quite oblivious to the music that had continued to filter up the building's stairway. But when Juan opened the front door, a blast of operatic sounds in the form of a chorus blew into the apartment with gale-force winds.

Unperturbed, Juan poked his head farther into the hallway. "*Turandot*," he said thoughtfully. "She just loves Puccini." Then, turning around and smiling softly, he added: "I guess this is her way of saying, 'Welcome to Lawrence, Massachusetts!'"

Chapter II

*O*nly a few weeks after the Cruzes arrived in Lawrence, Maria was hired as a machine stitcher at a clothing factory called Greco Brothers. She had never worked for a living before coming to the States; back in Cuba she had been a simple housewife and a mother. On setting foot in the U.S. and discovering her husband was living with a mistress, she was forced by life's circumstances to seek employment.

With watery eyes and a tremulous voice, she had asked her son Manuel to lend her the six-hundred dollars he had saved up (more on account of Mr. Strickland's insistence than out of his own free will) from his newspaper routes in Winnetka, Illinois. She had promised to start paying him back as soon as she started working and could save some cash.

Maria had answered an ad in the Miami *Herald* for machine stitchers in a clothing-manufacturing company in Opa-Locka. A picket line of striking men and women marching in front of the factory and bearing angry signs had hurled bitter insults at her in English and Spanish. Unflinchingly, she had braved the verbal barrage, broken through the line, and landed a job there. In just a few months, with the help of overtime work, she had paid her debt to Manuel in full. She had worked uninterruptedly at the Opa-Locka factory until coming to Lawrence. The management there had congratulated her for being an outstanding worker and had said that they would miss her.

It was in June that the Cruzes had arrived in Lawrence, but even though it was now only the middle of July, Maria asked Juan to help her find a Catholic school to enroll her sons in for the coming school year. Pablo and Juan first took the Cruzes to St. Mary's High School, where they were informed that, first of all, that particular institution had no grammar school and, secondly, it was an all-girls school run by nuns. Manuel had felt deeply embarrassed by the silly mistake. The Cruzes and Pablo left with the recommendation they should try Holy Rosary Grammar School.

An institution also managed by Catholic sisters, Holy Rosary Grammar School turned out to be what Maria wanted for her two young sons. Here a middle-aged nun greeted them with a courteous smile.

After introducing herself as Sister Georgina, principal of the school, she ushered them into a small office with a wooden desk and several uncomfortable chairs. For enrolling the boys in the school, she explained, she would need their vaccination papers and previous school records. Maria asked Manuel to tell the nun that it was no problem, that she had such documents. The nun went on to state what the tuition amounted to and how payments could be made.

Maria fell silent for a while, and during that time Manuel trembled inside, afraid his mother would unleash her haggling nature and demand a tuition reduction, citing that she was a poor Cuban refugee and a mother trying to raise two kids on her own. Manuel breathed more easily when he heard Maria say to him: "Ask her if she needs a deposit."

Manuel translated his mother's words from Spanish into English as quickly as possible, fearing his mother might change her mind all of a sudden.

"There is no need for that now," the nun answered. "She can give one if she wishes when she brings the documentation requested."

Just then a tall nun peeked into the principal's office. "Oh, I'm sorry," she said on seeing Sister Georgina had visitors. "It can wait. I'll come back later."

"No, it's fine, Sister Helen," the principal grinned. "You're not interrupting anything. Come in and meet one of your new students for the next school year: Manuel Cruz. He'll be in your eighth-grade English class."

Manuel stood up and shook Sister Helen's hand. Although she was tall and seemingly big-boned, her hand felt small and soft and delicate. He noticed her eyes were large and dark and beautiful. His heart fluttered for a moment.

"I hope you love to read," she said pleasantly with a smile that showed flawless white teeth. "I'm a very demanding English teacher." She winked mischievously at Maria and then gently ruffled Manuel's hair.

All of the sudden, some sort of volcano erupted inside Manuel and splashed burning lava all over his face and neck. He knew Sister Helen had seen the steaming blush, and the thought of this made him blush even more furiously.

"See you in September," she said gently, and swiftly

walked away, her long, thick skirts rustling deliciously like autumn leaves.

The new academic year began and in school Manuel could not help feeling immensely alone, especially during recess, when his lack of friends became most evident. Instead of joining the other students in their silly games and idle chatter, he would often merely stray off to a desolate corner of the school yard and lean with his back against a wall of the two-storied red-brick school building. At such times he would feel upon himself the curious, probing eyes of almost all the eighth-grade boys and girls near him.

To complicate things for him, the math taught by the tiny, emaciated Sister Imelda would often leave him utterly befuddled. In Miami he had attended Ada Merritt Junior High, a public school with a bad academic reputation. Obviously, the seventh-grade math taught at Ada Merritt, Manuel now confirmed, had hardly prepared him for Sister Imelda's more modern and advanced brand of mathematics.

"Manuel, do number seven," Sister Imelda shouted.

The explanation the nun had been developing on the blackboard in preparation for the book exercises had put Manuel's mind in a fog. Nonetheless, he struggled with the problem and blurted out an answer.

Sister Imelda's steely blue eyes turned icy-cold. "Mr. Cruz, have you started thinking about going to high school?" she suddenly asked with a sharp edge of sarcasm to her voice, a wry smile forming on her dry thin lips.

Manuel had overheard stories from other students

about the nun's limitless capacity for heartlessness and cruelty, so he now braced himself for the worst.

"Yes, Sister," he replied nervously.

"What high school, may I ask, are you considering attending?" she went on to say, rising from her chair behind the wooden desk and putting her hands on her hips in a challenging manner. Although her height barely scraped five feet, she suddenly loomed gigantic and menacing in her stiff black nun's habit. "That is to say, of course, if you do graduate from grammar school."

Canadian by birth, she spoke with a slight French accent to her English. To Manuel's ears, though, her accent seemed to have acquired additionally a sharply wicked tone.

Manuel heard a few giggles bubble up from the back of the classroom.

"Lawrence High School," he said hoarsely over the lump that had formed in his throat.

"Well, I believe you'd better reconsider," she said, the shadow of a smile flitting across her lips and presaging a concealed dagger of evil intentions, "and start thinking about Essex Agri."

The class now roared in unison with hysterical laughter.

His pride wounded by this hilarious avalanche, Manuel lowered his head, covered his face with a hand, and blushed uncontrollably.

During recess he wandered off in the school yard to a high-wire fence that enclosed the yard from a narrow alleyway, through which the food trucks came daily to make their deliveries to the school cafeteria. He looked morosely at everything and at nothing in particular in the alleyway, nursing the hurt in his ego. Suddenly, he felt a warm hand on his shoulder.

"I just finished correcting the grammar tests," Sister Helen said cheerily, "and you got a ninety-five. Congratulations," she grinned, and stretched out her hand.

Manuel shook it, noticing that, although her nails had no nail polish, they looked exquisitely delicate and feminine just the same. After thanking her, he gazed downward at the ground.

"Hey, don't thank me," the youthful nun said. "It was you who got the grade, brainy guy."

Manuel began to draw a circle with the tip of his right foot to fight off his growing self-consciousness and the rising flush.

"It's not good to look downward like that," he heard her say, feeling her hand gently lift his chin until his eyes met hers. "It's bad posture. It can ruin your spine. Now, put your head up and draw your shoulders back and act regally. Yes, *thatta boy*! Better, much better!" she beamed.

His heart hammered inside his chest as he studied her face. His eyes concentrated on her lips, which seemed quite sensuous despite the absence of lipstick on them. Her eyes were dark and warm and liquid, unlike Sister Imelda's, which were blue and icy and harsh.

"You know, when I was younger, my parents enrolled me in a modeling school," she said, her voice growing much softer, her big black eyes veiled by the thin mist. "Of course, that was before I entered the convent," she quickly clarified, perking up again. "Anyway, in modeling school I learned about proper posture in walking, sitting, even standing, and about proper manners. Most importantly,

I learned about treating people," she said, and smiled the sweetest, most wonderful smile he could remember ever encountering in his life.

"Oh," was all he could manage to say. But his head remained erect and high, and his eyes now fearlessly, unabashedly, confronted from a distance those very same eighth graders who just a while before had mocked him with their peals of laughter.

"Would you like to make a new friend?" Sister Helen presently said.

"Sure," Manuel replied.

"Frank!" she called. "Could you come here please?"

The student obediently trotted over to where Manuel and Sister Helen stood by the wire fence. It was obvious from the boy's way of running that he was not very well-coordinated or athletic.

"Frank, meet Manuel Cruz," the nun said. "Manuel, this is Frank Scuito."

Then she whisked herself away, her skirts making swishing sounds.

"You're the boy from Cuba, aren't you?" Frank asked.

"Yes," Manuel said, looking at Frank's ample nose as discreetly as possible.

Nobody in the eighth grade had a larger or more prominent beak. It was not only big and protuberant but also exaggeratedly curbed, like that of a parrot. Out in the hallways nicknames like "parakeet" or "Mr. Hook" could sometimes be heard aimed at Frank, who seemed to take the insults in stride, like water off a duck's (or parrot's) back.

"Live far from here?"

"Oh, no. I live just a few blocks down that way," Manuel said, pointing with a fully extended arm.

"What street?"

"Apple Street."

"By the Lawrence River?"

"Right."

Frank grinned. "Oh, I know where that is. Apple Street is exactly five blocks from here?"

Manuel nodded.

"And it's only two blocks long, dying at both ends?"

"Right."

"So that's where you live!" Frank exclaimed. "*Fangullo,* that's where that old geezer killed himself last year!"

Manuel shrugged his shoulders. "I wouldn't know about that. I moved into the neighborhood just this summer."

"That explains it," Frank said. "Well, at any rate what happened was this old Italian guy who lived around where you live—or maybe on the same street as you, if I recall correctly—blew his brains out. It happened about a year ago or so. It was a big thing around here because he belonged to the parish, you know, Holy Rosary Church. I think he had some strange disease or other and was under a lot of pain or something like that. Well, apparently, he was so unhappy and miserable that he decided to do away with himself. I would have done the same thing, wouldn't you?"

"I'm a Catholic," Manuel answered. "You go straight to hell if you kill yourself. If there's one thing I'd never do, it's commit suicide," he assured Frank in a very firm voice.

"Yeah, I guess you're right, looking at it that way. Anyway, I remember very clearly," Frank went on to say, "that Sister Helen asked us to say a prayer for the poor old man and she even shed a few tears in front of us. She said she was a friend of the widow and felt very sorry for the old lady."

"By the way, what's Essex Agri?" Manuel suddenly asked.

"I guess you don't want to talk about dead people, huh?" Frank smiled. "Especially if they kicked the bucket right in your neighborhood," he chuckled. "Really, I don't blame you. Anyway, what's Essex Agri, you said? Well, if I were you, I wouldn't worry too much about the incident with Sister Imelda. She's often mean and sometimes even *brutal*." Then he leaned in Manuel's direction and whispered: "She's a *real bitch*, if you asked me."

Manuel chuckled. "But what's Essex Agri?" he insisted.

"Oh, it stands for Essex Agricultural Institute," Frank explained. "That's where you learn to milk cows and raise chickens and shit like that," he said. "But don't worry. Sister Helen tells me she's sure you'll be going to Central Catholic."

"Central Catholic?"

"Yeah. That's the finest Catholic high school in Essex County."

Chapter III

"Could I help you?" said the blond young lady from across the counter.

"Is Mr. Tobias in?" Manuel said. "He recently called me. I think it's about a paper route."

"All right. Just a moment please. Your name?"

"Manuel Cruz."

The incessant clanking of typewriters being ferociously pounded filled the air in the huge room that enclosed the open front offices of the Lawrence *Eagle-Tribune*. One of the typewriters, he clearly noticed, was a black Underwood machine, like the one his father's secretary had typed on back in Cuba.

The room was divided into two areas. The area on the right as one entered the newspaper building from Essex Street was set off by a low wooden railing, had a plethora of desks and typewriters, and was apparently the newsroom and obviously the major source of the clanging noises. The area on the left was demarcated by a long, wide counter and served as the customer-service department as the sign on top of the big counter indicated.

Manuel remembered the afternoon when he and his

mother had been strolling down Essex Street, the main artery of Lawrence's downtown district.

Suddenly, as they had been about to pass the *Eagle-Tribune* offices, Maria had said: "Now that we're here, why don't you apply for a newspaper route? You've been telling me you were going to do so for I don't know how long. You can't depend on me for an allowance for the rest of your life, you know."

And days later he had decided to apply for an afternoon paper route.

"Mr. Tobias will see you now," the returning young woman said. "Come this way."

The wooden railing was L-shaped, meeting the long counter at the lower tip of the L. The blond-haired lady opened the railing door at the bottom part of the L and led Manuel to a partitioned office with a large glass window.

Mr. Tobias, a freckled red-haired giant of a man, squeezed Manuel's hand until a bone in it made a cracking sound. He asked Manuel to take a seat. On his desk a sign read: "Mr. Tobias, Circulation Manager."

Mr. Tobias went into the economic details of the paper route right away. Manuel listened attentively, nursing his crushed hand. Theoretically, Manuel could make, Mr. Tobias explained, about eleven dollars a week after paying for his papers (which would cost him 8 1/2 cents per unit and which he would sell for 10 cents per unit) and for his accident insurance, which was compulsory. He could increase his net profit, of course, by going after new customers and increasing his customer base, just as long as he did it exclusively within the limits of his route area. He would need a delivery bag with the *Eagle-Tribune* name and logo. This he could buy brand-new from the newspaper company for three dollars or second-hand from the departing newspaper boy at whatever price both boys agreed on.

Finally, Mr. Tobias asked if Manuel had any questions.

"When can I start?"

"If tomorrow the outgoing paper boy starts training you, the route will be formally yours on Monday." Mr. Tobias paused to clear his throat. "So whadda you say?"

"I'll take the route Monday and start training tomorrow," Manuel replied.

Mr. Tobias flashed a huge smile and rose to his basketball-forward height. He had to be, Manuel estimated, at least six feet six inches tall.

Mr. Tobias and Manuel shook hands, sealing the working relationship established. This time, though, the giant's handshake was much gentler. Mr. Tobias then offered to show Manuel where he would need to pick up his papers and led him toward the rear of the building. The circulation manager had to lower his head as he exited his office and later as he went through the double doors that led to a noisy, dark backroom.

Manuel was quickly assaulted by the pungent smell of ink and the deafening roar emanating from the running presses directly upstairs. A chute kept spitting out bundles of newspapers secured together tightly with metal wire, while a grubby middle-aged man stood at the mouth of the chute, catching the bundles and grunting out names and throwing the bundles either at the chests of the waiting delivery boys or onto the ground if no one answered the call—a clear sign that the paperboy hadn't shown up yet. In that backroom the noise level was so ear-splittingly high, the air felt so heavy and stuffy and foul, things all around looked so grimy and disorderly and gloomy, that for a moment Manuel thought he had walked into some sort of exploitative Charles-Dickens-type sub-world, akin to a factory or a coal mine, exempt from child-labor laws.

"This is where you'll pick up your papers Monday through Saturday," Tobias yelled above the mechanical din. "You'll also meet the departing delivery boy here tomorrow, oh, I would say, at about the same time as today. He's not here yet. But I'm sure he'll be on time tomorrow."

When Manuel got home, he told his mother what Mr. Tobias, the circulation manager, had informed him. She was pleasantly surprised at the amount of money he would be making.

Then her face clouded over and she said skeptically: "We'll see if this is true when you bring home the money."

The following day the outgoing delivery boy was a half-hour late. He made no attempt to apologize for his tardiness but merely said: "You must be the new paperboy. I'm Rick. Alright, pick up that bundle of newspapers and follow me."

Manuel threw the bundle on his back, like a young stevedore, and trudged after Rick. They exited the backroom of the newspaper building through a warehouse-type rollup door that opened onto an alley used by the *Eagle-Tribune* trucks to pick up bundles for drop-offs to those paperboys whose routes were too far away from the publishing plant.

At the mouth of the alleyway, Rick ordered: "Throw down the papers."

Manuel did as he was told.

"No, not on the sidewalk, dummy. Back here *inside the alley*, under the fire-escape ladder against the side of the building."

"But you said to throw down..."

"Never mind what I said. You don't want some s.o.b. catching sight of them papers a mile away, do you?"

The inappropriate use of the objective pronoun "them" when the demonstrative adjective "those" was called for—something he had learned well in Sister Helen's English class—told Manuel that Rick came from an uncultured background.

"Now, here, take these pliers and cut the wires."

"Where could I buy a pair like these?" Manuel asked, as he severed the wires. He began to bend and wind the wire around his hand, using his palm like a spool.

"I'll sell you mine for five bucks."

Manuel judged the price a bit high but didn't want to be blunt with his answer. After all, he had just met this rough-looking, uncouth youth and he needed Rick to show him the route and teach him the ropes.

"I'll think about it and let you know by tomorrow," he responded in a friendly tone and slipped the folded wire into his back pocket.

"Hey, what are you doing with that?" Rick demanded. "You stupid or something? It'll make a hole in your pants. Give it to me."

Manuel thought he had no other option but to obey. Rick was a couple of inches taller and at least two years older than he. On top of that, he looked like a tough guy who came from the slums where things were settled with the fists and not with peaceful logical arguments. And, worst of all, Rick had this constant I-don't-give-a-damn mean look on his acne-infected face. His glaring red pimples that peppered his countenance did nothing to make him appear less aggressive. His disarrayed spiky dirty-blond hair rounded out his appearance as a ruffian from the ghetto.

Manuel, thus, took the wire and gave it to Rick, who instantly threw it into the middle of the alley.

"That could puncture a tire on one of the newspaper trucks," Manuel observed. "They pass through here constantly, you know."

"And who the hell cares!" Rick laughed. "Hey, this frigging newspaper company has bled me enough!"

Manuel shook his head with incomprehension and shock.

"Alright, buddy," Rick then said, slapping Manuel on the back, "let's begin your training. Or should I say your education in the university of the streets?" He slapped Manuel in the same place again and handed him a filthy cloth bag with a long shoulder strap attached to it. "Okay, put fifteen papers in here. By the way, I'll also let you have the paper bag for an extra five bucks if you buy the pliers."

Manuel felt his intelligence insulted and didn't hesitate this time to reveal his opinion concerning Rick's latest offer.

"No, thanks. I can buy a brand-new one for three from the *Eagle-Tribune.*"

"Is that what a new one still costs? Fine, I'll sell you mine for three, too."

"But yours is used!" Manuel wanted to add "and filthy, not to mention stained and with holes!" But instead he kept quiet about the bag's other drawbacks.

"Jesus, what a wheeler-dealer you are! You must be

a frigging Jew! Okay, I'll make you a deal. You buy the pliers for five and you can have the bag for two."

"I'll let you know tomorrow," Manuel said diplomatically.

"Hey, kiddo, tomorrow may be too late."

"What do you mean by that?" Manuel said, suddenly feeling worried.

"Oh, never mind. Put fifteen papers in the bag, like I said."

"What are you going to do with the rest of the papers?"

"You ask too many questions. Just take the fifteen. No, make that seventeen."

"And leave the rest in the alley? What if somebody steals them?"

"Nobody steals from me, kiddo," Rick said menacingly, contradicting himself, in Manuel's mind, with his previous statement that someone could filch the papers if not well hidden. "I have a reputation, you see. Nobody wants to get his ass kicked in for messing with me. See the scar here." He pointed at a small scar just above his left eyebrow. "That's from a scuffle with a nigger who tried to run off with my paper-route money bag. The monkey cut me with his ring. But I beat the shit out of him and got this little thing back," he grinned, producing the zippered money bag from underneath the waistband of his trousers. "Okay, let's get moving. Shooting the breeze ain't gonna get this route done."

Manuel could not help feeling some admiration for the toughness of character Rick exhibited. Still, he sensed he was going to have problems liking the older youth.

In silence he slid his arm and shoulder under the strap of the newspaper-laden bag, hefted it off the ground, and followed Rick out of the alleyway and onto the sidewalk of the narrow side street. They headed in the direction of Essex Street, Lawrence's main thoroughfare.

"By the way, how do you know how many papers to take on a run like this?" Manuel queried. "And, also, how do you know how many papers to order for the following day?"

"You just play it by ear," Rick said nonchalantly. "That's all."

He had quickened his gait and had already gained a body's length on Manuel.

"Jesus!" Manuel said under his breath. Then, raising his voice, he cried: "Hey, listen, Rick, you can't leave me up in the air like this. How the hell am I going to take over this route if you don't explain things to me the right way from the very beginning?"

"Hey, settle down, settle down, kiddo," Rick ordered. "There ain't nothing to get upset about. You'll get to know the route in time. Just do what I tell you and you'll be fine. Okay?"

Trying neither to sound nor to look submissive, Manuel kept his face as expressionless as possible. "Okay," he answered in a firm voice

They entered Essex Street and Rick kept up his fast pace, bumping into several scurrying downtown shoppers.

All of a sudden, he halted and said: "Go up these stairs here and do the two offices on the right on the second floor. It's Friday, so it's payday. There'll be envelopes waiting for you with money. Pick them up and bring them to me."

"But aren't you coming with me?"

"Today is the most hectic day of the week on any

paper route," Rick explained. "It's payday, you see, so we've gotta split up."

"But how am I going to learn who all the customers are?"

"Just do as you're told and there'll be no problems," Rick said, his voice stiffening, his eyes turning cold. "Now, come on! You're wasting time!" He grabbed a couple of papers from the bag Manuel was carrying. "Go upstairs, get paid, and wait for me out here."

Manuel bounded up the stairs, hoping he could perform in record time what he had been asked to do. That way he might be able to catch up to Rick and learn who the other customers were. At both second-floor offices he was received with warm, friendly smiles and asked if he might be the new paperboy.

Handing him a heavy envelope with change, one woman at the second office remarked, "Hallelujah!"

"He's a handsome one," a second woman, with a high blond hairdo, remarked. "I hope he stays well-mannered and decent and doesn't start coming in later on with the smell of liquor on his breath like that bum Rick."

Both women laughed, and Manuel lost no more time listening to their jabbering. He flew out of their office and scuttled back down the wide staircase at breakneck speed, skipping two and three steps at a time, the coins clinking in his pants pocket, the bag flapping like a bulky cloth wing against his side. When he hit the sidewalk pavement, Rick was nowhere to be seen. Standing on the edge of the sidewalk and raising himself on his tiptoes while holding on to a parking meter for balance, he craned his neck and looked in all directions again. Suddenly, Rick popped out of a shoe shop, and Manuel rushed toward him.

"What stores did you do?" Manuel asked breathlessly, taking out of a shirt pocket the little green notepad he had brought to write down the names and addresses of the newspaper customers.

"Hey, get off my back! You're wasting time, and time is money."

"Just give me the names of the places you just did."

"Alright, alright, Capps and Lord's," he said, and then abruptly stopped dead in his tracks and struck out his hand, palm upward. "*The bread.* Don't make me have to remind you again, you hear?" he warned, his eyes darkening and narrowing.

"I forgot because you've got me running around from the very start like a chicken with its head out off," Manuel blurted out, handing Rick the envelopes with the money.

Rick flashed a smile. He opened the envelopes and started counting the cash.

Then suddenly a suspicious frown covered his face. "You didn't take any of the money, did ja?"

"Of course not," Manuel quickly responded, meeting Rick's probing stare unflinchingly. "The envelopes were sealed."

"Yeah, you're right. Jesus, then what a pair of cheapskate bastards! This kind of tip is something they should give a street beggar or a nigger, not their departing handsome, debonair white paperboy, who's busted his ass delivering their papers six days a week for two solid years. I mean, shit, I've caught colds and what not braving rain and sleet and snow under all kinds of weather to make sure those two hags got their newspapers! Heartless, thankless bitches!" He started walking down Essex Street again and then suddenly stopped dead in his tracks. "By the way, did that pair of slutty women say anything bad about me?" he asked with a very serious face.

"Oh, no," Manuel replied. "We had no time to talk."

"Good boy," Rick said, punching Manuel playfully on the shoulder over which the younger boy had slung the cloth bag with the papers.

Rick shook his head and bit his lips. Then he looked at Manuel and grinned in a strange way.

"Hmm, but that's okay. I'll get my going-away present one way or another. I don't care whose skin it comes off from!" He took another paper from Manuel. "Okay, let's shake a leg!" he said, and started trotting across Essex Street. "Do Look Photo," he ordered, pointing at the store on the other side of the street. "And don't forget to get paid!"

"Where are you going?"

"Sandler's," Rick shot back, and vanished inside the leather-goods store.

Manuel wrote down both names, did the camera shop, and flew out, payment in hand.

"Do Rose's Beauty Salon just up the street on this same side," Rick said, grabbing the money.

"And where are you going?"

"To the garage around the corner."

"What's the address of the place?"

"Stop worrying and do the beauty salon," Rick barked.

Manuel dashed up the street. He had difficulty opening the door to Rose's Beauty Salon and stumbled in, some of the papers spilling out of his bag.

"Are you the new paperboy?" a bosomy middle-aged woman with a high frosted hairdo chuckled in a deep, throaty way. "Bring the paper over here, son," she ordered, slapping the glass counter. "Ooh, a cutie," she cooed. After sliding him the money over the counter, she squeezed his cheek and said, "Now you slow down a bit and take good care of yourself, you hear? You don't want to hurt yourself, do you? My, my, you're gonna be a handsome man one day!"

He was quickly getting tired of the silly flattery about his looks coming from ladies who were old enough to be his mother or grandmother. He hurried out, red-faced, and jogged up the street and around the corner. He espied the garage and sprinted toward it. Rick was already strutting down the steep asphalt ramp.

"Did you do the beauty salon?"

"Here's the money!"

"Good!"

Manuel fished out the notepad from his pocket again.

"What's the name of this street?"

"Don't bother me! The tips are disgustingly miserable this week," Rick snorted. "What? Writing again? Damn it! Willja come on!"

By this time Manuel had decided arguing with Rick was fruitless and perhaps only served to get the older boy into a meaner mood. As long as he managed to end the day jotting down at least sixty or even just fifty percent of the names of the customers, he would be in good shape for the next day, when he would again be accompanying Rick on the route and could discover the existence of precisely those customers he might have missed today. So far, so good. Not a single delivery stop had escaped his notice, but he was sure that he would not be able to keep up for long with Rick's relentless pace. The gaps would soon start creeping into the route pattern he had been trying establish by jotting down as diligently as possible the names and addresses of the customers. Nonetheless, he could still look at the present state of things from an optimistic point of view.

Overall, the route looked very promising. A hefty portion of it was situated, according to information provided by Mr. Tobias, in the downtown area, a potentially plentiful source of future customers if Manuel played his cards right and treated his present customers with tender loving care and delivered the goods on time and if the official customers then spread the news he was an excellent person and an efficient delivery boy. He was really no neophyte at delivering papers; he had had afternoon and morning paper routes in Winnetka, Illinois. He would know how to get on the customers' good side right away, no sweat. Besides, he was a hard-working person by nature, like his mom, and would never be late on his route as apparently was Rick's custom. Also, he had never smoked or drank and wasn't planning to change his abstemious habit in this regard ever.

The rest of the route followed the same pattern of deliveries with Rick and Manuel splitting the customers about half and half. The only difference was that Manuel eventually started tiring while Rick's pace seemed to become more relentless and frenetic.

Consequently, Manuel started missing the names of some of customers being done by Rick, who showed great indifference at Manuel's predicament. On several occasions, however, Rick apparently could not help displaying a certain kind of satisfaction and glee over Manuel's suffering.

They worked the downtown area exclusively until the

final leg of the route, when Rick suddenly said, "You're going to enjoy this last part."

Chapter IV

$\mathcal{A}$s they began to trudge across an empty lot, Rick pointed toward a blue and white two-storied building that looked to Manuel like a small hospital.

"What is it?"

"A nursing home," Rick frowned. "Let's see how many old farts have croaked on me this week." He cleared his throat. "By the way, what's your name?"

"Manuel Cruz."

"Manuel Cruz? What kind of a name is that?"

"Spanish."

"You're a *spick* then! Oh, my God! I should have known! But you don't look the part with those blue eyes, white skin, and light hair. They threw me off!"

"I'm Cuban," Manuel corrected, although too tired by now to start an argument.

"Where do you live?"

"Apple Street."

"Hey, I used to have a route around there. Whadda you know!" Rick tilted his head in a reminiscing pose. "Matter of fact, I had a real weird bird of a customer right in your neighborhood. Her husband, I recall, killed himself or something. At least that's what the widow told the police afterwards. But, of course, nowadays you never know. I mean, the wife could have bought life insurance on the old hubby and then bumped him off, later claiming it was an accident or a suicide or something. Get the picture?" he said, winking at Manuel. "Besides, what prosecuting attorney was gonna wanna land a poor old widow behind bars? It wouldn't even look good on him. So he probably struck a deal with the old hag on the side and let her off the hook so she could collect on her husband's insurance and enjoy her last days splurging what she got from her poor husband's death. A fat bribe goes a long way, you know, and it never hurts anybody. In this case I guess it saved a wrinkled dinosaur from spending the rest of her life in the joint. By the way, is it dinosaur or dinosaur*ess*, if it's a female dinosaur, I mean?"

Manuel stared at the insensitive young man with forced indifference, a sharp hatred already beginning to simmer inside.

"But then how would you know about such things? You're a *spick*," he spat out, and laughed.

Manuel thought it wise to keep his mouth shut, but the repeated ethnic slur was becoming quite annoying and almost intolerable.

"I would appreciate it if you'd stop calling me that," he said through his teeth. "You can call me Cuban but not the other thing."

Rick studied the younger boy intently. Then suddenly he cracked a huge smile. "Now that was a ballsy remark! It shows character. Hey, I like that! I don't know why, but I like it. Tell you what, give me that newspaper bag. I'll help you with the rest of the route."

"Don't worry," Manuel said firmly. "I'm doing just fine."

"What? Are you kidding me? You look like you're ready to drop dead."

Only twenty to twenty-five newspapers remained in the bag. The total newspaper count in the original bundle had been seventy-five newspapers. Still, Manuel felt grateful for the kind gesture, even if it had come at the very end of the route.

"Strange. I don't remember ever seeing you around that part of town," Rick said as the started to trudge toward the main entrance to the old-folks home. "Around Apple Street, I'm talking about."

"I moved to Lawrence this summer."

"That explains it. Where did you live before you moved to Lawrence?"

"Miami. And before that, Winnetka, Illinois. And before that, Cuba. I came to this country when I was ten. I was part of a huge secret thing called 'Operation Peter Pan'. In fact, it brought to the U.S. thousands of Cuban children. *More than fourteen thousand*, I heard from my dad. At the time, of course, I didn't know it was called that. My father was the one who filled me on all of that. In any case, I came to the U.S. by myself."

"You mean, all alone, without your parents?"

"Yeah," Manuel said proudly, glad he had impressed Rick. "Oh, and by the way, Operation Peter Pan was run by the CIA and the Catholic Church."

Rick whistled. "What a combination, huh? So you must be a very important person."

"Not me. *My father.* He fought against Batista's government and then against Fidel Castro's," Manuel said breathlessly, as both adolescents continued walking toward the nursing home trough the vacant lot. "He's the one who got me into Operation Peter Pan. He worked for the CIA at the time—against Fidel, of course."

"So your father was a big shot in Cuba," Rick said, tilting his head to one side and looking at Manuel a little differently.

"Yeah, you could say that," Manuel replied, feeling prouder than ever of his father.

"But you said you came to the U.S. alone. You're not an orphan, are you? Your parents didn't die in Cuba, killed by Fidel Castro, did they?"

"Oh, no. My parents were able to leave Cuba a year and a half after I got out."

"Who did you live with while your parents were still back in the old country?"

"I spent about a month in an orphanage in Chicago until this institution called the World Catholic Organization found me an American family to live with."

"You mean, 'foster parents'?"

"Right, something like that. Anyway, their last name was Strickland."

"And you spent a year and half with the Stricklands, you said?"

"Yes. But it wasn't that bad because they had four kids, Christopher, Patrick, Anne, and Emily," Manuel fondly recalled. "That helped me blend in and feel at home right away."

"And now you're with your real parents?" Rick asked softly.

"Uh—huh."

"You're lucky," Rick said in a clipped voice. His Adam's apple rose and fell, and he bit his lower lip, which trembled a little. "I've been in and out of orphanages and foster homes as far back as I can remember," he added, sounding strangely hoarse. "I hardly remember my real parents."

Manuel felt he had suddenly stumbled by mistake on a dark and very intimate detail, in the same way one would accidently trip on a jagged rock in the middle of a rugged empty lot like the one they were presently crossing. In the thick silence that ensued, both he and Rick walked the remaining stretch of weed-covered, debris-strewn plot of ground. They entered the nursing home through a side door with a sign over it that read "Manor Home".

Manuel was immediately struck by the hospital-like smell, which, he gradually perceived, had a special edge to it, a slightly fetid odor that brought to mind images of rotting things. Instinctively, he associated this odor with the first handful of residents he saw. Through the corridors, gripping with arthritis-deformed, tremulous hands the wooden handrails running along the walls, shuffled, ever so slowly and feebly, haggard, bent old people, their eyes and cheeks sunken, their scanty hair disheveled, their emaciated arms sticking out like fragile dried twigs from loose greenish gowns, their shriveled thighs showing the stains of countless spidery varicose veins through areas in the gown carelessly left unbuttoned. Fighting the nausea that was gripping his stomach, Manuel recalled that from the outside he had thought the place some sort of hospital. Now it looked more like a morgue with miraculously walking corpses or a humane concentration camp or a graveyard full of ghosts.

Rick poked Manuel with an elbow in the ribs and Manuel was so startled he almost jumped.

"Whoa! There's nothing to be scared about," Rick said.

"These poor creatures don't bite, you know. Not at this time of day anyway. At nighttime, though, it's a different story. They turn into vampires," he said, showing his teeth like fangs and making his eyes big *a la* Bela Lugosi, "and then they go out and haunt people's sleep and dreams. So if in bed tonight you feel a heavy breathing on your neck, don't be surprised! It's one of them getting ready to suck away your blood!"

Manuel locked eyes with Rick for a moment, and then Rick threw back his head and roared with delight, his belly shaking with laughter.

All the compassion Manuel had felt for the confessed orphan went out of the younger boy at the sight of Rick making fun of helpless old people.

Two young nurses sauntered out of one of the rooms, and Rick quieted down. The nurses flashed smiles, and Rick waved a hand and beamed back coquettishly.

"Let me tellja something," he whispered to Manuel. "In this hell of a joint, the nurses are about the only nice things to look at. The rest just makes you want to puke. Arrgh!"

Manuel couldn't help chuckling softly. Indeed, Rick was right, he thought. Although he didn't know about the rest of the nurses, the two that had just crossed his path, in their spruced white caps and uniforms, with their springy gait, rosy cheeks, and lively eyes, did undoubtedly offer a most comforting as well as striking contrast to those deathly pale, decrepit ancient bodies still trying to defy the force of gravity while dragging themselves at a snail's pace along the endless corridor walls that seemed to lead to nowhere except the cemetery.

Rick's first delivery in the nursing home took him to a room where an old man lay supine inside an oxygen tent.

Thin plastic tubes ran out of his nostrils and a steady soft wheezing sound floated through the transparent tent walls. The other bed in the room, neatly made, yawned empty. Rick threw the paper on the vacant bed.

"Who's that paper for?" Manuel asked, taking out notepad and pen. He figured the owner of that particular newspaper was out of the room taking a stroll along the corridors of the nursing home.

Rick pointed with his chin at the old man probably inhaling his last breaths.

"You're kidding!" Manuel explained, flabbergasted.

"Quiet! You'll wake him out of his coma!" Rick snickered.

Then, in a more serious tone, he said: "To be perfectly honest, I don't think a paperboy should concern himself with what a customer does with his newspaper. He could use it to clean his behind, for all I care. As long as I get paid, I deliver and ask no questions."

"But..."

"But nothing! You see that old man right there looking so wasted away and innocent and helpless? Next week or the week after or the one after that, when he croaks and leaves you holding the bill and you go to the front desk to get paid and they tell you that they're sorry but the relatives left no money for you or his estate is tied up in court and all that crap, then you're gonna remember me and say, 'Christ, what a fool I was to have felt sorry for that old bag of skin and bones. In the end, the old geezer screwed me over good!'"

Something didn't make sense for Manuel. "So why deliver him the paper when you might not get paid."

He smiled maliciously. "His son pays me a week in advance, sometimes two weeks ahead of time."

"Oh," Manuel replied, but suddenly he did not feel very comfortable with the idea of Rick's having gotten paid ahead of the game.

Out in the hallway Rick said, "Did you see that empty bed next to Mr. Murphy's?"

"Is that the guy's name?" Manuel asked, pulling out his small notepad and a pen.

"Yes, yes. Did you see the empty bed? Well, it belonged to Mr. Carbonetti. He kicked the bucket last week. Guess what day he decided to die on, the son of a bitch? Thursday. That's right! On a Thursday! The day before payday! Can you imagine! Anyway," Rick sighed, shrugging his shoulders, "the result was another uncollectible added to my endless list of bad debts."

"I thought you said you got paid ahead of time in such cases."

"Not in *all* cases. Murphy is an exception. He looked healthy and all of a sudden croaked on me. At any rate, I suggest you listen to me and take my advice: Keep an eye on a geezer like the one we just saw and, when you see he's looking real bad and getting ripe to roll back his eyes, stop deliveries at once and run to get paid if he owes you money. If he doesn't, well, so much the better. You can still save money by returning the dead guy's paper to the *Eagle-Tribune*." He walked a few more steps, stopped dead in his tracks, and then said, swinging his outstretched right arm theatrically in an arc, "*Death is all around us, buddy*! Brrrrrrrrrr!" he said, shaking his hands as if he were trembling from cold fear inside.

Manuel didn't know whether to smile or to frown.

During the next dozen or so deliveries, no extreme case of physical infirmity comparable to Mr. Murphy's was encountered, to Manuel's relief. Then suddenly, as he strolled right behind Rick into a room, he caught sight of something that froze his breath in his throat. Sitting quite unashamedly as if everything were quite normal, an old woman lay fully undressed in a half-sitting position in bed. The upper half of a two-crank manual hospital bed had been partially raised, and she was leaning against it, looking as happy and innocent as an aged Eve resting comfortably against the trunk of a tree in the Garden of Eden. Her pendulous, withered breasts, reaching almost to the edge of her pubic triangle, hung like dried-out wineskins streaked with heavy stretch marks. In shock and disgust, Manuel turned around and quickly walked right back out into the hallway, leaving Rick alone to deal with the exhibitionist old lady, who had been holding an envelope, like a fallen apple, between her purplish thighs.

Rick came out counting the money with relish. "Hey, buddy, better get used to this sort of thing!" he growled. "They're people, too, you know, and, most importantly, they're customers. So what if sometimes you've gotta dance to one of their loony tunes. It don't hurt none," he grinned, slipping several bills into his money bag. "That old hag is by far my best tipper. I guess I should say 'was', right?"

Manuel looked away, getting even more disgusted with Rick's sarcastic opportunism.

When only two newspapers remained to be delivered, Rick and Manuel headed toward the end of a wing on the second floor of the nursing home from which the voice of a male singer softly drifted.

"Hello, Mrs. Di Giovanni. How are we doing today?" Rick chirped as he entered the last room on the right-hand side at the very end of the hallway. His mood had been growing more upbeat as he neared the termination of the day's deliveries. "By the way, Mrs. Di Giovanni, today it's my last day on the route, and I wanted to tell you how much I'm gonna miss your Italian music. You can't imagine how depressed I already am," he whined, furtively rolling back his eyes at Manuel while suppressing a grin.

"Oh, is that fact?" Mrs. Di Giovanni said with calm skepticism.

She put her knitting paraphernalia on the window sill and, without much effort, rose to her feet. Tall and erect, she walked toward the night table and took out a small purse from the drawer. As she paid Rick, she studied Manuel closely.

"You like Mario Lanza?" she asked Manuel.

"I'm terribly sorry but I don't think I've ever heard of him," Manuel said embarrassedly.

"That's him," she pronounced, tilting her grey head toward the record player by the big window.

Manuel lowered his gaze, concentrating on the musical sounds. He heard a vibrant, melodious masculine voice belt out:

Without a song
The day would never end.

"Well, what do you think?"

"Nice voice," Manuel said.

"Nice voice?" Mrs. Di Giovanni broke into a smile. "A *great* voice! The greatest since Caruso!"

She stretched out a hand, which Manuel shook, feeling the size and strength of it. Of all the old folks he had seen in the nursing home, she undoubtedly showed the greatest amount of physical wellbeing and mental sharpness as well as the fewest signs of the ravages of time.

"You must be the new paperboy," she said, again addressing Manuel.

Manuel nodded his head.

"I think we're going to be good friends," she assured him cheerily.

As he and Rick exited the room, Mr. Lanza boomed out:

I only know
There ain't no love at all
Without a song.

"Can't stomach that tomato-sauce wop music," Rick snarled, once in the hallway.

He knocked on the closed door right across the corridor from Mrs. Di Giovanni's room.

"Watch this," he warned. An impish light sparkled in his brown eyes. "Mrs. Cohen? Mrs. Cohen?"

"Yes? Who is it?" a hoarse, feeble voice answered from inside.

"Your son is here to visit you!"

"Oh, *gut*! How vonderful!" the voice exclaimed, acquiring a sudden brio and resonance.

"Should I let him in?"

"No please! Not yet! Not yet!" Mrs. Cohen cried, almost hysterically. "I must get dressed! I vant to look my best for him!"

Suddenly, Rick threw open the door, revealing an old woman who was still lying in bed and who now threw the bed sheet over her head. Like a frightened child or animal, she began to scream at the top of her lungs.

"Surprise! Surprise! It's your paperboy!" he shouted.

He then tossed the paper into the room and quickly slipped back out, slamming the door shut. "Scram!" he told Manuel.

With Mrs. Cohen's screams still going strong inside her room, the boys beat a fast retreat out a side exit door and down a wooden staircase.

"Didn't you forget to get paid from Mrs. Cohen?"

"The front desk paid me, didn't you see?" Rick said, still chuckling over his cruel joke.

"What's wrong with the woman?"

"Her son died in a war overseas, but the crazy bitch still thinks he's alive! I think she was in some concentration camp in Germany or something when she was a young girl."

God, what a sick thing to do to a old woman who had suffered so much! Rick should be in jail, Manuel thought. Then Manuel was struck by a suspicion.

"By the way, you told Mrs. Di Giovanni this was your last day."

"Did I really say that? Well, if that's the case, then it's time to say good-by, *spick boy*," Rick said, and then suddenly turned around and threw the paper bag at Manuel's chest. "From this moment on, the route is officially yours. Man, it feels so nice to know I'll never see those old farts ever again. Rick is a free boy from this day on!"

"Now hold on just one minute, Rick. The route isn't mine until Monday. Tomorrow I'm supposed to come along with you just to finish learning the odds and ends of the route. That's all. I don't have to do it by myself. As a matter, I don't have to do it at all."

"Well, then don't," Rick smiled maliciously. "That's my farewell gift to you," he added, pointing at the grimy newspaper bag. "You already paid for it anyway," he laughed, and started walking away.

In shock and disbelief Manuel watched Rick strut away with a jaunty step down the sidewalk until he turned into the vacant lot on the other side of the building and disappeared from sight.

Shaking his head morosely, Manuel started his long trudge home.

Chapter V

That night Manuel slept rather poorly. He turned and tossed in the sofa bed a good portion of the night as he mentally tried to retrace his steps through the paper route. With each failed attempt of his to reconstruct the route fully in his mind, he felt more and more anguished and tortured. It was like being trapped in a phantasmagoric maze.

The following day, however, he did not do as badly as his nightmares had indicated. Still he missed around fifteen customers. Right after finishing the route, he went directly to see Mr. Tobias, who was sympathetic and told him not to be concerned.

"The customers you missed will be calling later today or Monday morning," the circulation manager said gently. "We'll explain to them, of course, why their paper wasn't delivered. By Monday afternoon at the latest you should have all their names and addresses, and with that your customer list will be complete."

In that respect things turned out, more or less, as Mr. Tobias had predicted. On Friday, however, just when Manuel thought that at last he was in the full swing of things and everything was going hunky-dory, he learned

Rick had stabbed him in the back in yet another way. Apparently, under the pretense he was going on vacation for a week and was leaving a replacement he didn't fully trust, he had demanded a week's payment in advance from a certain number of customers, predominantly coming from the ones he had done alone the previous Friday without Manuel's presence.

Luckily, not every customer he had approached with his ploy had fallen for it. Still the total losses Rick had caused him amounted to at least eleven dollars, approximately the sum of his profits for a week's worth of lugging and delivering newspapers. That meant he had delivered newspapers the first week for free.

He finished the route later than usual since it was payday.

Knowing the *Eagle-Tribune* offices would be closed by then, he went straight home. As he tiredly and dejectedly began the long climb up the staircase to his brother's third-floor apartment, he heard something creak behind him. Swiftly swinging his head around, he managed to catch a split-second glimpse of the old woman from apartment 1A as she hurriedly shut her front door.

Inside the apartment Maria scolded her son for allowing such a *pícaro* to fool him. "*Eres un tonto,*" she said pointedly. "You're a foolish boy. You have a lot to learn from life."

Later that night Manolo called from Miami, and Maria jumped on the opportunity to inform her husband of his son's business blunders. When Manuel came on the line, Manolo chuckled gently, "So the little gringo burned you, huh?"

"How was I to know," Manuel said defensively, annoyed that his mother had such a big mouth, "that he was pulling a fast one on me? I'm going to complain to the circulation manager tomorrow. Maybe he can do something about it."

"Remember: Don't get angry, just get smart," Manolo counseled. "What you're going through is painful, my son, but keep in mind that there's no better schooling than what you get from the University of Hard Knocks. That's where I got my best education, believe me. Going through that sort of school puts hairs on a man's chest." He laughed softly again. "Now, if you really want to improve your education further, you should start reading the master as soon as possible."

"And who would the master be?" Manuel inquired.

"Niccolo Machiavelli."

"I think I've heard of him." Manuel had never heard of the guy but didn't want to sound ignorant over the phone.

"The author of *The Prince* is my bedside bible," Manolo said.

"I'll try to borrow the book at the Lawrence public library," Manuel promised, although thinking that this Machiavelli fellow could not be greater than Dante.

"I thought you would have read him by now, scholar. Anyway he was a Florentine, like your literary hero. What's his name?"

"Dante Alighieri."

"Right. Tell you what? I'll send you a copy of *The Prince*. Consider it a gift from me to help you ease your entrance into the University of Life."

Early Saturday morning Manuel dropped by the *Eagle-Tribune* downtown offices.

"What brings you here so early?" Mr. Tobias inquired,

probing Manuel's face with friendly blue eyes. "I hope everything is going smoothly for you now."

"Not really," Manuel said rather curtly. "Rick got paid in advance for this week from several customers, and they say it's not their fault it happened. My loss totals over eleven dollars, and so I was wondering," he said hesitatingly, gulping down a dry lump that had formed in his throat, "if... if perhaps my insurance covers such a loss."

Mr. Tobias coughed into a fist. "I'm afraid not. The insurance you buy is accident insurance, which covers only physical accidents or injuries on the job. It doesn't cover monetary losses."

"Oh, I see," Manuel said in a disappointed voice that almost cracked. He lowered his eyes and thought for a moment. He was about to give up on the matter and beat a retreat out of Mr. Tobias' office when he suddenly remembered the previous night's telephone conversation with his father, who had advised him to get smart, not angry. His ears rang with his dad's throaty laughter. "Well, then, should I tell those cheated customers that they have to pay up again because it was their mistake, not mine?"

"Oh, no," Mr. Tobias swiftly replied, waving a thick hand in the air. "That's the last thing you would want to do. I mean, it could alienate or, worse still, deeply upset some of these customers. They might end up either cutting back on their tips to you or simply cancelling their subscription altogether. The latter result would affect us both."

"I see your point," Manuel quietly agreed. "But then perhaps the *Eagle-Tribune* could call Rick and put pressure on him to return the money."

Mr. Tobias interlaced his fingers over his prominent belly. "I don't think it'd do much good. Rick would vehemently deny any wrongdoing on his part. I know him well enough. Besides, he's no longer a paperboy and so we don't have any control or influence over him anymore. The only real solution to this dilemma would thus be to take him to court, and that could get really sticky and messy as well as drawn out and expensive—and for only *eleven dollars.*"

"To me that means a lot," Manuel retorted. He sighed deeply. "Then what can I do?" he asked in an anguished voice, a sense of hopelessness overwhelming him.

"Nothing, I'm afraid. I promise you, though, that I'll do everything in my power to help you increase the number of customers on your route. That reminds me, uh... I have a message here somewhere from a lady called, uh... Let's see. Now where is it?" Mr. Tobias muttered, rummaging through a tall stack of papers on his desk. "Oh, here we are," he said, brightening up and waving, like a small victory flag, a pink piece of paper, the type used to take telephone messages. "This lady called, as I was saying, but she didn't give her name, just her address. She said she wanted to start receiving the paper, provided you were the delivery boy. Now how do you like that? It's been only a week since you started on the job and already you're making quite a name for yourself, son!" He chuckled pleasantly, his protuberant belly rising up and down. "Anyway, according to the address given, she's actually outside the boundaries of your route, but since I want to make it up to you for what's happened on account of that scoundrel, I tell you what: I'll make an exception to the rule here and let you have her as a customer." He stretched out a long, hairy arm and handed Manuel the pink piece of paper. "Here's her address."

"Thirty-three Apple Street, Apartment 1A," Manuel read aloud. "Gee, that's on the first floor of the apartment building I live in!"

"So much the better. You can drop off her paper when you get home from the route. Nice, huh? By the way, she wants to begin receiving the paper right away. So start her off on Monday. Congratulations!"

During the weekend Manuel had nightmares in which Rick had returned to haunt him on the route. In one of them, Rick pilfered Manuel's papers left behind underneath the metal fire-escape ladder in the alleyway half a block away from the newspaper publishing plant. In another he went to see Manuel's customers and told them that Manuel had just quit and he was again taking over the reins of the route and was there to collect all due monies.

All during the route Monday, Manuel soothed his mind by daydreaming up all kinds of clever strategies for avenging the wrongs Rick had wreaked upon him. On his trek home, he delighted his imagination by wondering about just where in Dante's Inferno (if such a place existed) Rick would one day end up. He figured Rick would undoubtedly be damned to Circle Eight Bolgia Seven, where thieves were hurled to suffer eternal torture with their larcenous hands bound forever. He experienced a special joy when he pictured Rick being bitten in the neck by a huge snake and then bursting into flames and crumbling to the ground in a heap of ashes.

In such a frame of mind he knocked on the front door of apartment 1A at 33 Apple Street.

Everything being so perfectly quiet inside the apartment, Manuel wondered if anyone was home. He remembered this was the place through whose front door quite often opera music would emanate. While Pablo frequently accused the old woman who resided there of being off her rocker and being a nuisance with her loud operatic sounds, Juan defended her by saying she was just a quaint, sweet old lady who deserved respect and tolerance on account of her advanced age and solitary condition.

Manuel was about to drop the paper on the doormat and leave without confirming the new subscription, when suddenly he was struck with the thought that the mysterious call to the newspaper could perhaps be another of Rick's pranks. After all, the caller had not given a name, only an address. And, oh, what a strange coincidence that the address given over the phone led to an apartment in the same building Manuel lived in!

Manuel knocked a little harder on the door the second time. Still no sounds of movement came from the inside. Growing impatient, he pounded the door with the open palm of his hand. Almost immediately a soft pattering of feet was heard.

The door opened slowly to only a crack, and Manuel partially saw the face of an old woman, whose most prominent feature was her nose. It may have been a fine, noble Roman nose in its better days, but obviously, under the unforgiving weight of the passage of time, her snout had deteriorated considerably. Warped and wrinkled, it now looked about ready to collapse on a moment's notice, like an ancient bridge.

"I'm sorry I knocked so hard," Manuel said, slightly

embarrassed. "But I wanted to make sure you had ordered the paper."

The old woman smiled faintly and pointed at her left ear. "*Mi scusi. Non odo bene.*"

With the aid of his Spanish, he thought he had understood her: She was excusing herself for being hard of hearing. *Non odo bene.* The equivalent in Spanish was: *No oigo bien.*

"Oh, I see," he said.

She opened the door another crack. The apartment was quite dark inside, and in her pitch-black dress she seemed to form part of the deep shadows filling the house.

"*Parli italiano?*" she asked, her eyes twinkling like weary stars against a night sky.

"Oh, no. Not really. Ah, and here's your paper, ma'am."

Manuel extended the newspaper toward the door opening, but the old woman did not take it.

"You did order it, didn't you?" Damn, had Rick tricked him again?

Her gaze appeared to go through him and to get lost somewhere behind him, somewhere distant and in the past.

"Oh, *si, si,*" the old woman abruptly answered, breaking off from her strange daydream and grasping the paper.

Deeply relieved, Manuel started walking up the staircase. He had not climbed three steps when he heard her speak again.

"You like operas?"

He turned only his neck. "Operas?" He cleared his throat. "I've never listened to one, so I really can't say."

She opened the door a little wider. From his angle he could now see that her hair, splotched with grey, was pulled into a bun held together with a small curved ornamental comb.

She looked at him fixedly with a pair of big dark eyes, which suddenly softened to the point of almost seeming to smile. "I have many, many opera records. One day when you have time, you come and listen to a little piece of one," she said, raising a hand and indicating the extent of the measure with her index finger and thumb. "*D'accordo?*"

"*De acuerdo,*" he replied in Spanish, a smile breaking on his face.

Well, maybe the old woman was a bit strange, but somehow, unwittingly, she had managed to help him forget, although for just a brief moment, Rick's hateful face.

Suddenly, the lady started giggling, softly, happily, covering her mouth with a hand, like a shy young girl.

"*De acuerdo,*" she repeated in Spanish, and closed the door softly.

Chapter VI

" orry to interrupt the homeroom period," Sister Georgina said over the PA system, "but could all the eighth-grade homeroom teachers bring their students to the auditorium immediately for a brief assembly?"

In the auditorium Sister Georgina, better known as "Mother Superior" at Holy Rosary Grammar School, told the students that the applications for Central Catholic had arrived. Those considering attending this extraordinary Marist high school, she said, should ask their parents to fill out, sign, and return to their respective homeroom teachers the application forms, along with the application-fee payment. On the thirtieth of the following month, she also announced, the entrance exam would be administered at the Central Catholic auditorium.

For appearance's sake Manuel went up to the front of the auditorium and picked up an application package from Sister Imelda, who seemed to wrinkle her lips with annoyance on seeing him walk up.

On his way back to his homeroom classroom, he was approached by Sister Helen, who smiled and said, "I'm glad to see you're applying to Central."

"Well, I'll have to talk to my mother first," he quickly said. "And my father, of course," he added without catching his breath.

"Do you foresee any particular problems?" she queried.

Manuel lowered his eyes. He was becoming more aware with each passing day that Sister Helen had a significant ability to unnerve him.

Clearing his throat, he said: "Not really."

"You're not worried about passing the entrance exam, are you?"

"No. Uh, yeah, *that's it*. I really don't want to throw good money away on something that's so chancy."

She probed him with her eyes. "Do you need a scholarship to go to Central?" she asked point-blank.

"Well, gee, I dunno," he stuttered embarrassedly. "I've heard Central is quite expensive. I'll have to ask my mother—I mean, my father."

"Tell you what. Fill out the application forms. Then return them *directly to me*," she said, pointing at the crucifix hanging on her bulging chest. "Not your homeroom teacher." That was Sister Imelda. "Furthermore, disregard the application fee. It'll be taken care of somehow. Now, you got all that down?"

He nodded his head, enthused with the idea of going to Central.

"Good," she said, and touched his shoulder gently, a caring smile blooming on her face.

On unsteady numb legs, Manuel walked away and stumbled into the wrong classroom. When he noticed it was not his homeroom, it was too late: the eighth-graders there had burst into laughter.

After school he went home to pick up his paper-route bag. He left the high school application on top of his mother's dresser. It was payday, and so he trudged back home late in the afternoon with the sun already sinking behind the tops of houses and apartment buildings while drenching the sky with a dark bloody color.

When he knocked on the door of apartment 1A, he heard the sounds of music coming from the interior. He waited a discreet amount of time and then began pounding the door.

Soon he heard the tenant's voice cry out: "*Vado! Aspettati un momento!*"

Dressed in black, the old woman opened the door. He clearly remembered she had appeared dressed in the same color on the first day he had delivered her paper as well as on occasions when he had seen her dropping her correspondence off in the mailbox around the corner. Maybe she was in mourning, he thought, for some relative of hers who had died recently.

"It's collection day, ma'am," Manuel said gently.

"Oh, yes, of course," the old lady replied, smiling without showing her teeth. "I be back." She shuffled away and returned with two one-dollar bills.

"It's only sixty cents," he corrected her.

"I know. But you take the two dollars," she said, pushing the bills into his hand. "Through the window I watch you coming home every day after you deliver *i giornali*. You look very tired. You look like you work very hard. You take *il denaro*. It is not much. You deserve. You take."

She closed his fist and pushed away his hand.

"Oh, thank you," he beamed. "Thank you very much."

"In Italian you say, '*Molte grazie*.'"

"*Molte grazie*."

"*Prego*." She cleared her throat. "You like the music I play?" she then said, opening the door a little wider as if to allow the musical sounds a freer outward flow.

"It's nice. What is it?"

"It's an aria from *Il barbiere di Siviglia*, a comic opera. Perhaps you want to listen to just a little piece of it," she said to him, smiling her closed-mouthed smile and, like on their previous encounter, forming with her index finger and thumb a sort of U bent sideways to express graphically the smallness of her request. "You promised. *Ti ricordi?*"

"Yes, I remember," he grinned.

"Come on in then," she said cheerily. "*Avanti. Avanti.* I prepare for you *un caffè di expresso delizioso*. You like Italian coffee, yes?"

"If it's like Cuban coffee, I'm sure I'll like it," Manuel said, stepping inside.

The old lady's apartment, like the inside of a movie theater, seemed enveloped in deep shadows. He had to allow his eyes time to adjust to the darkness before he was able to discern anything. He followed the black figure of the old woman, who apparently, like an aged cat, felt quite at home in such gloom, showing little difficulty in finding her way.

Slowly, he made out the thick curtains covering the parlor windows. Through a thin crack between the curtain folds where the window blind had been partially raised, a tiny sliver of dying sunlight broke through, striking a dust-filmed, cobweb-covered piano, which seemed to have remained closed and untouched for a thousand years.

The old woman turned on a light in the kitchen, making it easier for Manuel to cross the living room. The music seemed to be coming from one of the bedrooms. She now moved in that direction, dragging her feet. The volume was turned up, and Manuel thought he recognized the present tune:

Ehi... Figaro... Son qua.
Figaro qua, Figaro la,
Figaro su, Figaro giu.

When she returned to the kitchen, he said, "I think I've heard that song before."

"It's a very famous aria," she informed. "You like to sing?" she asked, turning on the burner where a coffeepot sat.

"I've sung in church choirs," he informed her. "In Winnetka, Illinois, I even sang a solo once in a solemn mass. My music teacher then thought I had a good voice," he said with pride. "I was an alto."

"I'm very happy to hear that," she responded cheerily. "Very, very happy. Have a seat, please. Maybe I give you singing lessons. You want? I am a voice teacher."

"Oh, gee, thanks, but I'm too busy right now with the paper route and school work."

"Maybe during summer vacation?"

"I'll think about it," he said neutrally, not knowing what else to say.

"I charge *nulla*. I give lessons for free."

"That's very kind," he said, but he refused to commit himself.

When he was seated in one of the dinner-table chairs, she went on to say: "I used to sing, too. I was an opera singer. *Una diva. Una prima donna*," she pointed out, suddenly straightening up her back and making a grand gesture with a hand. Delicately, slowly, she let her hand fall, like a wilting flower, her back assuming its former curvature. "Of course, that was *molto tempo fa*. A long time ago. A *very* long time ago." She shrugged her shoulders and smiled her tight-lipped smile, returning her attention to the coffee being brewed.

"Hmm. Interesting," Manuel remarked, running a hand over parts of the large wooden table, which felt quite smooth and solid and clean. After she served him the coffee, she sat across the table from him and asked him about *la scuola*.

While Manuel informed her that he was attending Holy Rosary Grammar School, where he was an eighth grader, she listened to him, subtly cupping her right ear with a hand.

"You go to high school after?" she asked, making small circles in the air with the hand that had been cupping her ear.

"Oh, yes, ma'am."

"Lucia," she corrected softly. "Lucia Farfalla. Many, many years ago it was Madama Lucia Farfalla. Now, sometimes, it is Madama Butterfly," she giggled, shielding her mouth with a hand.

Although the kitchen was dimly lit with just about all natural light being blocked out by closed curtains and lowered blinds, he still managed to catch a fleeting glimpse of those gaps in her mouth that meant missing teeth and molars.

"Madama Butterfly?" he said, wrinkling his brow.

"Well, yes, that's what the neighborhood kids call me once in a while. I explain. One day the landlady comes to collect rent and she knocks on my door and cries very loud, '*Madama* Butterfly! *Madama* Butterfly!' You see, she knows I play the role of Cio-Cio San in the opera *Madame Butterfly* in Milan *molti anni fa*. Well, one kid hears her and tells all the other *bambini* on the block. A few days later when I go mail a letter, a bunch of *ragazzi* follow me and suddenly start chanting, '*Madama* Butterfly! *Madama* Butterfly!' I pretend I hear nothing, and then they shout, 'Oh, *Madama* Butterfly—she's deaf!'" She giggled behind her hand. "And they stop and go away, leaving me in peace."

"Have they called you that again?"

"Only a few times more. But the other day when I go to the mailbox, a few *ragazzi* yell at me, 'Witcha! Witcha!' That I did not find so funny," she grimly observed.

Manuel shook his head. In silence he finished his coffee.

It tasted like Cuban coffee, he thought, except that it was less strong and not sweetened as much.

"And so you know what high school you go to next year?" she now asked, trying to revive the previous conversation.

"Not really," he confided. "One of my teachers, Sister Helen, well, she wants me to go to Central Catholic, but it's a very expensive school."

"Oh, I see," Madama Farfalla said, lifting her head up and down very slowly a couple of times.

The music record had come to an end, and Madama Farfalla struggled to her feet and shuffled off as quickly as her old bones could carry her. When she returned, Manuel had risen from his seat and picked up his paper route bag.

"I gotta go now," he said.

"You like *Il barbiere di Siviglia*?"

More music commenced to drift in from the room.

"Oh, gee, I dunno."

"*Il barbiere*—that means 'the barber'," she explained. "My husband—may his soul rest in peace—he was a barber. When he sees me for the first time, I am singing the part of Rosina in *Il barbiere* in an opera house in Napoli. A wonderful coincidence, *non e vero*?"

Manuel nodded his head. "It's getting late. I must leave," he now said with more conviction.

"You come back some other time and listen to a little piece from another opera, yes?"

"Sure," he said tiredly.

As they went through the living room, she caught him looking in the direction of the piano. With the aid of the artificial half-light splashing into the parlor from the kitchen, he was now able to discern two dust-covered articles lying next to each other on top of the black piano. In a macabre way the mirror and the dagger seemed enmeshed and bound together by a thick common cobweb. He couldn't understand why she kept the dining table so immaculate and the piano so filthy.

"I don't play the piano anymore. Since *il mio marito* died, I don't play it, I don't touch it, I don't dust it," *Madama* Farfalla explained, as if having read his thoughts. "Nothing. *Nulla*. My husband—he loved to hear me play. Now when I go near it, I feel a big *dolore* inside here," she said, touching the left side of her chest with a closed fist while bowing her head. "The dagger belonged to my father, the mirror to my mother. I keep them over the piano because la *musica* sometimes, like a mirror, reflects the heart and sometimes... sometimes, like *un pugnale*, stabs *il cuore*," she said in a whisper, closing her eyes and suddenly plunging into her chest an imaginary dagger in a theatrical way. With her eyes still closed, she sighed deeply. Then, as abruptly as she had made the violent hand gesture, she shook her head and, opening her eyes wide, chirped, "Forgive this ancient lady. Old divas are very dramatic people. We carry the disease of tragedy in our blood and in our heart. You forgive? Yes?"

"It's okay. I understand," Manuel said, although not really knowing what to make of all that. He speedily stepped out into the hallway.

"You come back some other time?"

"Sure, no problem," he said, and bounded up the stairs to his older brother's apartment.

Chapter VII

The day the Central Catholic entrance exam was going to be administered fell on a Saturday. Since Juan was free from work that day, he offered to drive his half-brother to the high school.

In the car Manuel began to whistle an aria from *Il barbiere di Siviglia*. He felt happy and at the same time confident he would do well in the entrance exam.

"Are you starting to like opera music?" Juan said. "You play that *Il Babieri* LP record so often, it'll soon wear out."

Manuel chuckled softly.

"Is it a gift from Madama Farfalla?"

"Uh-huh. She's a little bit weird, but she's nice and even kind of funny. Every Friday when she pays me, she asks me to come in and have an espresso coffee with her and 'listen to a little piece from an opera'," he said, imitating her accent and her gesture with the hand and two fingers.

"Do you remember when back in Cuba I would disappear all of a sudden for several days and grandma would tell you I had gone out of town?" Juan said, taking his eyes off the road for a moment and casting a glance at Manuel. "Remember?" He gently poked an elbow into Manuel's ribs. "You should because back then you'd immediately ask grandma for permission to let you use my bike. Am I refreshing your memory or what?"

Manuel felt his breath get caught in his throat. Relief came when he saw a smile break on Juan's face.

"My God, when did you discover that?" Manuel chuckled. "I was so secretive and careful about the whole thing. Did grandma blow the whistle on me?"

"Never," Juan laughed, "because, you see, I was the one who told her to let you use my bike. As a matter of fact, I even asked her to suggest the very idea to you!" He now shook with laughter as he glanced sideways at me.

"You're pulling my leg, right?" Manuel cried out, feeling utterly confused. And during all those years, he had thought Juan resented him for some strange reason.

"No, it's the absolute truth! I knew my father wouldn't allow you to have a bike. I also knew you wanted one very badly. So grandma and I conspired together to make things a bit more pleasant for you," he beamed.

"Hey, thanks," Manuel said with difficulty. "That was a very nice thing to do on your part."

Jesus, to find out something like this after so many years left one practically speechless.

"So every time you took my bike during those times, you thought you were doing something bad, huh?" Juan asked gently.

Manuel nodded his head bashfully.

"Sorry about that. I didn't mean to deceive you. It's just that my father—or should I say more appropriately, *our father*—was, and forgive me for saying this, a complete idiot. You know what I'm mean?"

Manuel didn't know what was more appropriate for

the occasion: to nod in agreement or to remain quiet in response to his older brother's question. He opted for staying still and mute.

"Anyway, do you know where I used to go on those trips?" Juan went on to say.

"No, not really. I have no idea."

"*To see operas!*" Juan exclaimed.

"Operas? You're kidding me."

"No, it's the absolute truth. I would go to see them at the Grand Opera House in Havana."

"Hmm, that's amazing. But then why don't you go to operas anymore? Aren't there any opera houses in Boston?"

"Oh, of course, there are. It's just that... well, times change and one changes with time, and, besides, seeing a performance might bring back too many memories, good and bad, and that can kill you inside."

"Madama Farfalla would probably agree with you a hundred percent. She says music is like a mirror and like a dagger."

"Plenty of daggers in operas."

"Oh, yeah?"

"Yes, like in *Carmen* and *Otello* and *Tosca* and *Lucia di Lammermoor* and *Madame Butterfly*"

"Lucia! That's Madama Farfalla's first name! She used to be an opera singer. At least that's what she tells me."

"She was?" Juan said, slowing down for a yellow light. "I thought she was a music teacher. At least that's what the landlady once told me. Well, what do you know! A former diva living right in our apartment building? Does she still sing?"

"She's too old for that now, I guess. Besides, she's deaf in one ear or something like that, I think."

"No wonder she plays those opera records so loud!"

"Tell me, what's this *Lucia di Lammermoor* about?" Manuel inquired.

The car came to a complete stop before the red light.

Juan proceeded to explain that it was a story about a lady named Lucia who was forced to marry a man she didn't love. The problem was she had promised her love for eternity to someone else, whose name was Edgardo. On the wedding night, in a fit of remorse, she lost her mind and stabbed her husband to death. This happened off stage. When Lucia stumbled onto the scene, her white gown and hands were blood-stained. Her hair was all disheveled, and her eyes looked wild. She was still holding the dagger she had just used to kill her husband, whom she didn't love, of course. Soon her lover Edgardo learned of the tragedy and then of her death, and he, in turn, pulled out his dagger and stabbed himself, while singing he would join her in heaven.

The light turned green, and Juan's foot slid over to the accelerator, and the car lurched forward again.

"Man, that sounds so damn crazy and tragic, but it's interesting, I suppose," Manuel remarked tepidly.

"There's a lot craziness and tragedy in operas alright. And don't forget the daggers and the blood and thunder."

"Maybe I'll ask Madama Farfalla if she's got this opera *Lucia*. If she does, I'm sure she'll lend it to me."

"Go easy on the operas," Juan warned.

"Why?"

"Operas can be very interesting, that's for sure. But they can also be very intoxicating."

"I don't get it."

"You will one day," Juan replied with a wan smile.

"Opera exaggerates life. The problem comes when life tries to imitate opera." He paused and was silent for a while. Then he said: "I'll tell you something I've never told anyone."

Almost uncontrollably, Manuel felt himself begin to fidget in his seat. The thought of a possible moment of intimacy with his older brother seemed to strike a chord of discomfort deep inside him.

The first opera Juan ever saw was one composed by a great Italian genius named Giuseppe Verdi. It was called *La Traviata*. It was about a high-society courtesan named Violetta that met a young man called Alfredo who fell madly in love with her. At first Violetta rejected his advances, letting him know she didn't believe in love, only in pleasure, but eventually she fell in love with him, too, and gave up her trade, moving with him into a country house away from the hustle and bustle of Parisian high circles.

One day when Alfredo was away on some business matter, his father showed up at the villa and asked Violetta to make a great sacrifice and give up Alfredo, because her scandalous affair with him was ruining his sister's chances of marrying properly. At first Violetta refused to agree to do so, but finally she allowed herself to be persuaded to make *il sacrificio*, the sacrifice, and left Alfredo. When Alfredo saw her again at a ball, he insulted her, since he didn't know the true motive for the breakup. He exited in a huff and embarked on a trip. During all this time, Violetta had been suffering from tuberculosis and had been getting sicker and sicker. In the final scene, when she was on her deathbed, Alfredo returned, by now fully informed of the truth and her sacrifice. He poured out his love to her in song. But it was too late, and she died moments later, after giving him a memento to remember her by.

"Gosh, that's a complicated but very beautiful story," Manuel admitted. "Is there a moral to this story?"

"Yeah, that you shouldn't judge anyone too harshly, especially when it comes to things of the heart."

"Hmm."

"Anyway, getting back to what I wanted to tell you: At the time I went to see this opera, I was still in the seminary studying to become a Jesuit priest. Immediately after that operatic experience, I got hooked on operas and started sneaking out of the seminary when I was supposed to be engaged in spiritual exercises or doing meditation or simply studying," Juan chuckled. "In a way I'm glad all that happened, because, you see, I found out in time that I wasn't made out to be *un sacerdote*. Holy orders, I guess, had never been meant to be my cup of tea. On the other hand, the world of opera kind of screwed up my mind and almost led me to do something unspeakable."

The shrieking of tires suddenly split the air, knocking the breath out of Manuel's chest. Through the corners of his eyes, he saw a dark vehicle headed for a collision with his brother's car. Instinctively, he gripped the armrest, bracing himself for the impact. Miraculously, however, the impact never occurred. The two cars, his brother's and the other braking vehicle, somehow avoided each other by inches. The sounds of an angry klaxon and cursing voice followed the two half-brothers up a quarter of a block.

"Jesus, that was damn close!" Manuel exclaimed. "You know something," he said in a whisper, "you ran a red light."

"Oh, I did?" Juan said, as if still half lost in thought.

"Anyhow, as I was saying," he went on, giving the impression the recent incident mattered as much as the spilling of milk, "becoming an opera junkie almost made me do something I would have regretted the rest of my life. I could have even gone to prison for it!"

"What did you almost do?" Manuel asked, turning around and sneaking a look through the rear window to make sure the upset motorist or a police car with flashing red and blue lights was not in pursuit of them.

"*I almost murdered someone!*" Juan confessed, his jaws tightening, the knuckles of his hands turning white from gripping the steering wheel so hard.

"*What?*" Manuel cried in shock.

Had he heard his brother right? Had Juan, a former Jesuit seminarian, tried, in the distant past, to kill a person?

"Opera is an extravagant art. It puts one's emotions dangerously on high gear," Juan pointed out. Then he sighed painfully before going on to say: "I had just returned to Caibarien from Havana, where I had gone to see *La Traviata* for the sixth or seventh time. I was riding my bike on an errand when all of the sudden I saw Valeria."

"And who might she be?" Manuel said a little impatiently. His curiosity aroused, he wanted Juan to hurry and finish the story before they arrived at Central Catholic High School, where he would be taking his entrance exam that morning.

"My father's mistress."

The words roared and echoed in Manuel's heart like cannon fire.

Juan saw her and then noticed the coming bus. All of a sudden, something flashed and thundered in his brain, and the next thing he knew, he was pedaling hard and throwing his bike's front tire against her body. He knocked her off her feet, thrusting her out of the sidewalk and onto the street. She screamed as the bus tires shrieked. Then, scared like hell, he darted away on his bike. He pedaled so fast he almost smashed into a truck a block away.

"Did she get hurt?" I knew she was alive and well and living with my dad in Miami.

Juan's face had tightened into a pale mask; his lips were trembling slightly. He shook his head with a jerky motion.

"Did she report you to the police?"

As if momentarily speechless, Juan shook his head again.

"Did she tell my father?"

"No," Juan said hoarsely.

Manuel's mind was telling him to leave things as they were and stop the questioning, but his heart wanted one more answer. "But what did the opera have to do with what you did?"

Juan bit his lower lip and for a moment slumped in his seat behind the driving wheel. After regaining his original posture, he said: "I was terribly mad at this woman because she couldn't be like Violetta, because there was no nobility in her soul as in Violetta's case. She wasn't willing to make *il sacrificio* and leave her own Alfredo, our father, alone."

Both brothers fell into a troubled silence that lasted until they arrived in front of the entrance to Central Catholic High School.

"When do you want me to pick you up?" Juan said.

"Thanks, but it's okay," Manuel answered, getting quickly out of the car. With his feet on solid safe ground, he noticed he could breathe more easily. "I'll walk home."

"It's a long walk," Juan said with the saddest eyes.

"I don't mind," Manuel replied firmly. "I need the exercise."

Chapter VIII

During the following weeks, Manuel entered a state of heightened expectation. Every time he heard the neighborhood dogs bark, he would quickly look out through the living room window of his brother's third-floor apartment to see if the animal sounds were signaling, as they often did, the arrival of the mailman. The mailman had once explained the dogs barked when they smelled his sweat.

Presently, having heard the barking and espied the postman from the apartment window, he ran down the two flights of stairs and waited for him by the tenants' mailboxes near the narrow entrance door to the apartment building.

The mailman, a black man in his late twenties with afro-styled hair, entered the building, whistling a jazzy tune. "What's happening brother?" he said cheerily on seeing Manuel.

"Nothing much," Manuel responded. "Have something for me?"

"Just hold on a second there, my man," the postman replied, hand-picking the mail from his leather bag and slipping a batch of correspondence wound with a thick rubber band into one mailbox and magazines and envelopes into several others.

"You like to write, young cat?" he suddenly asked with a smile, as he slipped a couple of letters into the mailbox marked 1A.

"You mean, at school?"

"No. I mean letters. Do you like to write letters?"

"Not really," Manuel laughed. "I had to do so much letter-writing at one time, I got sick of it."

He remembered that, when he was living with the American family in Winnetka, Illinois, he had been forced by Mrs. Strickland to write his mother a letter every other day. He had hated the assignment immensely at the time. After a while, he had had to start inventing things to finish his letters to his mom as he progressively began to run out of things to write to her about.

"Hmm, I see," the mailman said thoughtfully, puckering his thick lips. He seemed to wonder about what I had just said. "Weird," he then muttered.

"Weird? What's weird?" Manuel asked, while searching with avid eyes for an envelope bearing the Central Catholic High School name in the mail the black man still held in his hands.

"Oh, never mind. It's none of my business anyway," the mailman said mysteriously. "Besides, I could get canned from my job for prying."

The African-American mailman handed Manuel several envelopes.

"Thanks," Manuel said.

As he climbed the stairs, he fingered through the mail, spotting the Central Catholic envelope. Out of breath and perspiring slightly, he entered the apartment, threw the other correspondence on the kitchen table, and prepared to open the envelope that enclosed part of his future. There was no one at home except himself. His younger brother Esteban was outside playing with neighborhood friends, and neither his mother nor Juan nor Pablo had yet returned from work.

He was glad for the privacy of the moment. With tremulous hands he tore the envelope open and pulled out the letter. He read quickly, skimming over the insignificant parts in search of the heart of the matter. When he found it, he read it again, this time much more slowly and carefully. When he was sure he understood correctly the decision of the school in regard to his application with a basis on his entrance-exam scores, he started jumping up and down, letting out whoops of victory.

"*Felicidades*, but how are we going to afford such an expensive school?" Maria said when she got home from work and heard the news.

Manuel felt as if someone had pushed him into a tub full of icy water.

"Sister Helen told me not to worry," he replied in a raspy voice.

"And who's this Sister Helen? Does she own Central Catholic?" Maria said, pursing her lips. "Does she run it? She's not even a Marist Brother!"

"But she's a Catholic nun," Manuel shot back, although without much conviction. "Alright, I'll talk to Sister Helen tomorrow," he conceded, and went back to reading his book on the kitchen table, feeling crushed.

As soon as he trudged into Sister Helen's classroom, she lit up with a broad smile.

"Hey, congratulations!" she cried happily.

"Thanks," he mumbled.

Not knowing how to begin and feeling awkward and a bit nervous, he let his jaw drop.

"Something troubling you?" Sister Helen said.

"Well, it's just that..."

"Yes...? Oh, I know. Tell you what," she chuckled. "Let's make it official. Could you bring your parents tonight at around eight?"

"Well, my father is living in Miami," Manuel said, blushing slightly, "but my mother and older brother could come."

"Excellent," Sister Helen said. "In the meantime keep that chin up, you hear?" she added, raising his face with a hand to meet her soft, liquid almond-shaped eyes.

Although Pablo offered to come along, Juan told him in a rather gruff voice that the subject to be discussed at Holy Rosary Grammar School was strictly family business.

Pablo didn't seem to take the brush off very well. He raised his eyebrows and was about to say something when he apparently decided against it and spun on his heels and left the apartment, closing the front door a bit too roughly.

It was practically obvious to everyone that, as of late, things between Juan and Pablo had gotten a little tense. From Juan's tone of voice in telling his friend Pablo not to meddle in his family's business, Manuel could tell the situation between the two friends had not improved one bit. On the contrary, the two men appeared headed on a collision path.

Sister Helen greeted the Cruz family with a radiant smile at the convent's front door.

"I'm glad you all could come," she said pleasantly, and led them through a vestibule into a reception room, where the four Cruzes, including Esteban, Manuel's younger brother, squeezed onto a single sofa, while Sister Helen sat down on an armchair.

The nun went right into explaining the main reason for the suddenly arranged meeting. A generous wealthy person had expressed the desire to pay for all of Manuel's expenses at Central Catholic High School during his full four years there.

Sister Helen paused to allow Juan to translate for Maria, who responded she would like to know the identity of the kind, noble-hearted person.

The nun smiled gently and shook her head. "Impossible," she said. "Such a request cannot be granted, I'm afraid. The benefactor demands absolute anonymity and secrecy in the matter."

Again Juan translated into Spanish what Sister Helen had said.

Maria practically did not let him finish.

"*Pero por qué? Es absurdo!*" she complained, directing her words more to her stepson, it seemed, than to the nun. "Listen, Juan, you tell the good sister I'm not interested in the person's or organization's name. All I want is some sort of an idea as to who or what the benefactor might be. I mean, is it a religious order, like the Marist Brothers? Or is it the parish? Or is it a single person? A man? A woman? I need to have some sort of idea. Please explain this to her."

Juan translated, and again Sister Helen shook her head, this time the smile being wiped off her face.

"The only information I can furnish is that all of your son's academic expenses, in terms of tuition, books, fees, etcetera, at the mentioned academic institution will be taken care of during Manuel's four years of study there by the benefactor, who, as I previously pointed out, wishes to remain *perfectly and absolutely* anonymous. And please pardon me if I'm being redundant."

For a moment there, it seemed to Manuel that Sister Helen was sarcastically implying that it was his mother, not the nun, who was being "redundant".

Once more Juan served as interpreter going in his stepmother's direction.

"Well, okay, tell her I accept the benefactor's condition of complete anonymity," Maria conceded at last with a tentative smile. "However, I would like some sort of guarantee that one day, out of the clear blue sky, maybe five, ten years from now, the benefactor won't suddenly show up and demand full reimbursement plus interest for all the expenses incurred in providing my son with a Catholic high school education."

Sister Helen listened to Juan's explanation patiently and then replied she would ask the principal Sister Georgina to write a letter stating that Holy Rosary Grammar School, the intermediary in this philanthropic transaction, confirmed that the money used to subsidize Manuel's high school education for four years at Central Catholic would be awarded by the benefactor on a fully gratuitous and non-reimbursement basis.

Maria seemed fully satisfied with this, and so everyone rose to their feet and Sister Helen, beaming a wide smile, shook hands with all the Cruzes.

"You've got a bright one there," she told Maria. "He'll make headlines one day. The sky's the limit for him."

That night Manuel had trouble falling asleep. Exciting new things were happening in his life. He was on his way to the best high school in Lawrence, and, furthermore, Sister Helen had said that he was bright and the sky was his limit. He felt euphoric, with all kinds of thoughts and dreams running amok through his brain.

One mental image, like an obsession, seemed to come back to him again and again: Sister Helen's glorious beautiful face.

While she had spoken to his mother in the convent's reception room, he had fixedly, obsessively, watched Sister Helen's lips. Somehow they had triggered the memory of Mrs. Strickland, his temporary "foster" mother while he had been living at her house in Winnetka, Illinois. On a certain Mother's Day, Mrs. Strickland had kissed all her children one by one smack on the lips. When she approached Manuel with her lips puckered, he puckered his, too. He had even closed his eyes to intensify the ecstasy of the moment. In his mind's eye, he had imagined her moist red-painted full lips coming into full contact with his. He could see them drawing near as they glistened like the luscious crimson pulp of a *mamey* fruit. When he had felt only a soft peck on the cheek, he thought he would faint, so heavy was his disappointment.

Slowly, achingly, Manuel's mind now returned to the convent and Sister Helen. While there, he had suddenly become aware of his arousal. Ripping his eyes away from Sister Helen's face and mouth, he had immediately begun to think about other things, things that would take his mind off the gorgeous angelical nun and help him cool off his feelings before his erection became stiffer and was noticed.

Hours later, in the dark privacy of the convertible

sofa in the living room of his older brother's apartment, Manuel felt he could give free reins to his imagination and emotions. Of course, he would have to keep his hands under wraps. As long as he didn't touch himself, there'd be no sin.

Or would there be?

Could not the mind sin as much as the hands? He wasn't sure, so he'd have to ask a priest about it one of these days in confession. In the meantime, just to be on the safe side, he'd better start saying a few Hail Mary's until he calmed down a bit and began growing drowsy.

Chapter IX

"Hey, young man!" Both Manuel Cruz and Frank Scuito stopped dead in their tracks at the sound of the booming voice and swung around quickly on their heels almost in synchronized fashion.

"You're calling me, Brother?" Frank said, pointing at his chest sheepishly.

"No. I want the student in the chino pants," the short, big-bellied, bald elderly Marist brother thundered. "Come over here," he said in a heavy deep voice.

"Yes, Brother," Manuel said, his heart hammering in his chest.

"Didn't you know you're not supposed to come wearing that type of pants to this school?"

"No, sir, I didn't. I'm sorry, Brother."

"You're supposed to wear trousers. Do you know what they are?"

"They're pants, Brother," Manuel replied, his voice quavering a bit.

"Pants with belt loops and leg cuffs! I want to see you wearing trousers tomorrow, young man! And they better be *dark* trousers, not light-colored like those chinos," the seemingly pugnacious brother warned. "And don't forget the belt! Is that perfectly clear?"

"Yes, Brother. I'm sorry, Brother," Manuel repeated, and walked away, his legs feeling like butter.

"Man, I thought I was dead," he said to Frank seconds later, without looking back at the religious executioner he had just encountered. "He made me feel for a moment there like I was a criminal or something."

"That was Brother Marcel, the Assistant Principal and Disciplinarian," Frank grinned.

"Oh, wow!"

As the two freshmen passed by a blue-eyed, sandy-haired lay teacher standing in the hallway just outside the open door of a classroom, Manuel heard him say, the hint of a mischievous smile flitting around his mouth, "You boys have to wear trousers, yet he can wear long ugly skirts, and he's not even a *Scotsman*."

The two boys chuckled nervously and went on their way.

"Who was that?" Manuel asked Frank, when they were some distance away from the teacher.

Since their days at Holy Rosary Grammar School, where they had also been school companions, Manuel had become aware that Frank had a special talent for finding out things before anybody else did. Classmates there had often kidded Frank about this ability of his by saying he a "nose" for things in clear reference to his enormous hooked Roman beak.

"Mr. Devlin, an English teacher," Frank answered. "We might get him for English this year. I've heard he's really witty and entertaining in class."

"He seems like a nice guy," Manuel commented.

"But I've also heard some bad things about him," Frank added, lowering his voice.

"Oh, yeah? What things?"

"That he's an atheist and that he drinks a lot and smokes pot," Frank informed almost in a whisper.

"Oh, God!" Manuel exclaimed.

Staring at Frank's huge curved nose and thinking for a moment that perhaps it had grown so big because Frank suffered from a mild form of Pinocchio's famous tendency to lie, Manuel speculated that perhaps his friend might be exaggerating just a tad.

Manuel and Frank had discovered to their mutual contentment that they had exactly the same class schedule. During lunch break that first day of regular classes at Central Catholic, both freshmen engaged in a lively discussion about the possibilities of their getting Mr. Devlin as a teacher.

"I heard he teaches a ninth-grade class in the afternoon. I bet you anything it's our class," Frank said, caressing his very thick black eyebrows that met right at the top where his jumbo nose rose like a small boat sail. One of his various nicknames was One Brow on account of the fact both brows of his made one continuous furry line at the bottom edge of his forehead. Apparently, from time to time, he would become so self-conscious of this facial detail that he would shave the spot over his nose to separate the brows, only to force his friends to veer toward other sobriquets like Captain Hook or Vacuum Cleaner.

Mike Bloom, a rare Jewish student in the Central Catholic freshman class, commented, "Don't be so sure. There are other English ninth-grade classes in the afternoon. Besides, he also teaches seniors. It could be a senior English class."

Mike was sitting next to Manuel at a cafeteria table. He had a strong nose, blue eyes, a high forehead, and wavy black hair. His mouth was small and narrow. The two adolescents had become acquainted for the first time during math class that morning, and since then both had tended to gravitate toward each other.

"It wouldn't make any difference," Frank replied. "He teaches only advanced classes, advanced seniors, advanced juniors, advance sophomores, and advanced freshmen, which is us."

"Is our homeroom an advance class?" Manuel asked, surprised.

"Of course," Mike Bloom replied with a proud smile. "Out of the six freshman homerooms in the class of '69, only two are advanced classes. We belong to the elite, Manuel!" he said, giving Manuel a congratulatory tap on the shoulder.

"Gee, whadda you know!" Manuel said.

After he had finished the sandwich his mother had made for him, Manuel crumpled the brown paper bag into a ball and said, "If, as you say, Frank, Devlin is an atheist and all that, why would you want him as your teacher?"

"Because he's funny as hell," Frank replied immediately. "You never get bored with that dude."

Mike nodded his head in agreement.

The three freshmen walked into English class together. They sat close to one another and waited for the arrival of their instructor. The second bell rang, announcing that their future teacher was officially late.

About three minutes afterwards, Mr. Devlin sauntered in, carrying a load of books under his arm. He plopped them down on the teacher's desk. A paperback spilled onto the linoleum floor, but when a student made a move to pick it up, Mr. Devlin's hand shot up, holding the freshman back.

Then, looking at the class with a half-taunting smile, the English teacher said: "What's that?"

He pointed but did not look at the floor. Instead, he scoured the class with a pair of intense, fiery blue eyes.

Someone raised his hand and answered, "A book!"

Soft snickering came from the back of the class.

"You're blind!" Mr. Devlin shouted, forcing quite a few heads to snap up as if someone had cracked a whip or lit a firecracker. He put his hands on his hips, pushing back the flaps of his navy blue blazer. "And you know why? Because your other eye, the eye that sees much more than your two physical myopic ones, is completely shut, like those on a newborn babe. And that's precisely the eye I want you to open. *The third eye!*" he almost shouted, suddenly bunching all his fingers of his right hand and tapping them against the very center of his forehead, over which a few strands of dirty blood hair fell. "So open it right now and see that there's much, much more to that book than a mere agglomeration of printed 5 ½ by 8 ½ inch pages glued together in perfect bound."

He paused and panned the class again with piercing eyes, while running a hand through his light-colored hair to push back the few fallen locks away from his broad forehead.

If Mr. Devlin had been a student and not a teacher, it would have been a sure bet, Manuel thought, that

Brother Marcel would have forbidden his entrance into the school until he cut his hair to a "decent" length.

A pin could have been dropped in the hallway, and it would have been heard in the classroom, so absolute was the silence among the students. In fact, it appeared as if every freshman in that English class had even ceased breathing for several minutes.

"Alright, listen," Mr. Devlin said, easing the pressure by smiling slightly and looking away through the large window that faced the cement basketball court outside. "If you're going to open your third eye, you're going to have to learn, first of all, to relax, you hear?" he counseled gently. "I mean, look at you. Right now you all strike me as a bunch of babies about to pee in your pants and inundate the classroom with your urine."

The class tittered spasmodically, knowing well that their new teacher had struck a truthful chord.

"So to soothe your nerves and get you warmed up to things, I'll answer my own question. If you look at that thing lying on the floor with that special eye, the eye of your inner being, you'll start seeing it as a living thing, as a pulsating world, a timeless universe, as... well... as *God!*" he said, his voice rising in crescendo. *"En arche en ho Logos, kai ho Logos en pros ton Theon, kai Theos en ho Logos."*

Students turned around and looked at one another, hunching their shoulders as an indication that they didn't know what the hell had been said or even what language the strange words came from.

Mr. Devlin spun around quickly, like an adroit dribbler going for the hoop, and approached the blackboard. He seized a yellow chalk as if he were grabbing a small sword and started writing in fast, hard strokes letters and words that seemed to come from some distant or alien civilization.

υ ρχ υ Λ γος, κα Λ γος υ πρ ς τ υ Θε υ, κα Θε ς υ Λ γος.

"Does anybody knows what this means," he asked, probing the class with ardent eyes.

The students remained mute and paralyzed.

Mr. Devlin shook his head and then said: "Okay, geniuses, here's the translation: 'In the beginning was the Word, and the Word was with God, and the Word was God.' Now, Einsteins, who put the words in that book?" he inquired with great force, pointing at the book on the floor but without glancing at it.

Nobody answered. Everybody seemed to have turned into statues under the violent, volcanic stare of the questioning teacher.

"I'll ask again: *Who wrote the words in that book*?" he now shouted.

Manuel raised a bashful hand.

"Yes, you!" Mr. Devlin said, his face lightening up.

"A man wrote them," Manuel said in a soft voice. He already suspected where Mr. Devlin was trying to take the issue.

"So if a man put the words there and the New Testament teaches us that the Word is God, then what is the author of that book on the floor?"

Manuel closed his eyes and lowered his head, fearing he would be asked to answer the frightening question.

"You!" Manuel heard the teacher say.

Manuel opened his eyes and saw Mr. Devlin was pointing at him.

"What's your name?" he demanded.

"Manuel."

"Full name, please," he said, softening his voice.

"Manuel Cruz," Manuel said, his voice almost cracking.

"I like your first and last names, Mr. Manuel Cruz," Mr. Devlin beamed in a cheerful voice. "Both are full of significance. Manuel means 'God is with us' and Cruz, obviously, comes from the Latin word *crux*, which means 'cross', an obvious reference to Christ's cross. So, Mr. Cruz, you have a divine name from any angle you look at it."

Manuel started blushing, while on his back he felt the hand of Mike Bloom, who with gentle taps was trying to give him encouragement.

"Okay, now, bright chap, please answer the second question. If a man put the words in a book and Christianity teaches us that the Word is God, then what is the book's author?"

Manuel wanted to get Dr. Devlin's attention off himself as soon as possible, so he gave a rapid answer: "The author is a sort of god."

"Of course! It's a matter of absolute logic, the conclusion of a simple syllogism," Mr. Devlin cried happily.

Students looked at one another in awe and consternation.

"Another question. How many minutes was I late?" He proffered the broadest smile. "What? You didn't notice?"

Giggles.

"Alright, I admit it. I was exactly three minutes late. Now what's three minutes?"

"A hundred and eighty seconds," someone said, and shrunk behind another student as if afraid of an imminent blow to the head.

"Use your third eye, goddamnit!" Mr. Devlin demanded. "What's a second? Come on, don't be afraid! I'm not

Count Dracula trying to suck the last ounces of blood left in your benumbed anemic brains, for crying out loud!"

Laughter from the class and a roguish smile from Mr. Devlin.

"What's a *goddamn* second?" he repeated with greater emphasis.

The same student who had given the previous answer proved relentless, coming back for more possible humiliation.

"A unit of time?"

"Are you asking me or are you telling me? Come on. Resuscitate your dead brains. What's a second? Alright, let me give you a couple of hints. What's a second in the mind of God?" Mr. Devlin said, punctuating the word "God" by opening his arms and throwing them wide apart, like the unfolding petals of a huge flower wanting to drink light from the sun.

The whole class seemed frozen by the enormity of the question.

"*An eternity,*" Mr. Devlin finally said in a soft whisper. "And that's exactly how long you've been waiting for me," he added with a strange smile, opening his arms again, "or for any other person, for that matter, who suddenly enters your life. So live your life according to the sacred importance of every person who walks into it and for every moment that is endless and infinite."

The class was left dazed.

Mr. Devlin proceeded to pass out the course syllabus, being careful to point out that no one should get obsessed with it, as in the short or long run he went about things primarily according to how "the spirit" moved him. This statement, uttered so nonchalantly, had the effect of disconcerting the freshmen students even more.

"At any rate, tomorrow we start with Shakespeare's *Romeo and Juliet*," he said. "So read the first act tonight."

During the next several days Mr. Devlin was the hot topic of conversation among his freshmen students in the school cafeteria.

"How old is that guy?" somebody wanted to know at the table where Manuel was sitting.

"He's in his thirties."

"Late thirties, I heard, although he doesn't look it."

"My father is in his late thirties and Mr. Devlin looks ten years younger."

"That's because Mr. Devlin's got lots of hair and your father is as bald as a billiard ball, you nincompoop. On top of that, your dad looks like Uncle Fester in *The Addams Family*, while Mr. Devlin has the good looks of Robert Redford."

Everyone at the table roared with laughter, except for the student whose father was the butt of the joke.

"An upperclassman told me Mr. Devlin just turned thirty-nine," a plump freshman with puffy rosy cheeks interjected. "Mr. Devlin confirmed this himself. He also said he was going to have a good year this year because the numbers three and nine were magical."

"I talked to a senior who had Mr. Devlin last year," Frank Scuito broke in, scratching his hooked Mediterranean nose, "and he told me Mr. Devlin's been married four times. Imagine that!"

The rosy-cheeked, corpulent freshman named John confirmed the information by nodding his head. "And he's got kids with every one of the four."

"Awesome, dude!" said a tall blond-haired freshman

who had a reputation for being a lady's man. "He's a veritable Arab sheik. He's got a harem! Lucky dude!"

"But Devlin doesn't live with all four at the same time, or does he?" Frank asked, his eyes wide with astonishment and disbelief. "He'd have to be a Mormon to be able to do that."

"Or a Muslim," Mike Bloom, the Jewish student, said.

"He's none of these things," John, the fat kid, interjected. "Besides, having a harem is illegal in the United States. What I meant was Mr. Devlin has married four times and divorced the first three wives. Oh, and by the way, the last woman he married was an Indian," he added, and took a huge bite from his sandwich.

"An American Indian?" Mike asked.

"No, an Indian from India," the overweight freshman explained. "She was a Hindu or Buddhist or Muslim or something like that. In any case she belongs to one of those godless pagan religions."

"What do you mean by 'godless' and 'pagan'?" Mike questioned, his voice bristling.

"That it's not Christian, that Jesus Christ is not at the center of it."

"Those religions you mentioned are not 'godless' or 'pagan'," Manuel said, getting into a discussion that he felt was really none of his business. He was intervening only to prevent a potential confrontation between Mike Bloom and the chunky freshman whose first name was John but whom most students called Porky. "I don't know much about those other three faiths, but I know for a fact Jewish people believe in a God, even though they don't believe in your Christ as the Messiah."

"And how do you know this, may I ask?" John said, beads of sweat breaking out on his forehead.

A big smile had bloomed on Mike's face.

"Well, because I read a good deal," Manuel replied, more than willing to defend good friend against an ignorant foe. "And so I know what you're saying is way off the mark." He then looked at Mike Bloom.

Mike gave him the broadest smile he had ever seen on the Jewish student's face, while Porky looked away, obviously reluctant to get into a verbal fight over the topic of religion.

During a recreation period later that day on the school's outdoor basketball court, Manuel learned from Frank that Devlin wrote on the side. A poetry book of Devlin's had been published when he had been a grad student at Berkeley. Also, he had had short stories published in magazines. He had even written a sales brochure on coffee for a coffee-importing company he had worked for before coming back to teaching. Supposedly, as a coffee salesman, he had travelled all over Canada and several regions of the U.S.

If Frank ever achieved his dream of working for the FBI, Manuel mused, he would surely make a pretty good G-man. Indeed, he had a sense of smell for a good scoop as huge as his rather prominent proboscis, perhaps a direct inheritance from Julius Caesar.

"So he's done other things to make a living besides teaching, huh?" Manuel said.

"Oh, God, yes! As a matter of fact," Frank said, "he came back to teaching only three years ago."

"Incredible!" Manuel said.

"What made him come back?" Mike Bloom queried.

"Ah, that bit of info," Frank replied, waving a knowing finger like a Sherlock Holmes lecturing a couple of 'dear' Doctor Watsons, "I pried out of a former Centralite who graduated last year and had Mr. Devlin precisely the year he returned to teaching. The explanation Mr. Devlin gave to that year's class was: 'I finally found my father and, thus, found myself. That journey has ended, and I have started a new one.'"

"Hmm," Manuel said.

"Deep," Mike remarked, nodding his head up and down.

"Very *Devlinesque*," Manuel returned.

"Hey, I like that term," Mike beamed.

"So you know what the students from that graduating class started saying?" Frank went on to explain. "That Mr. Devlin had been trying to find himself by looking through his third eye and into the belly button of his new belly-dancing Indian wife."

The three boys, Mike, John, and Manuel, broke out in chuckles.

John stopped the chuckles when he broke the news to his schoolmates that Mr. Devlin's Indian wife was sick.

"Oh, God," Manuel lamented, "what kind of sickness has she got?"

"I don't know exactly," Porky admitted. "All I know is her illness is terminal."

At that moment Frank Scuito made the sign of the cross over himself.

One Friday afternoon Mr. Devlin began class by asking: "What do I mean when I say that 'libido' prevails over 'credo' in *Romeo and Juliet*?" ·

"What does libido mean?" a student inquired.

"Libido is the life force, the sexual impulse or passionate element in man. It is, in brief, the love principle."

Another student raised his hand. "And credo?"

"That's Latin for 'I believe'." Mr. Devlin shook his head. "Start taking Latin classes, son. You don't know what you're missing." He opened up his arms wide and raised his head, as if he were looking at the heavens through the classroom's ceiling. "Oh, why, oh, why, my God, do I waste my genius in this desert air?"

The whole class roared.

"So libido over credo means love over belief, right?" asked Mike Bloom.

"Correct, Mr. Bloom," the teacher replied. "So how is libido over credo, love over belief, exemplified in this tragic play of Shakespeare's?"

Mike's arm shot up again. "Well, it's the deep love Romeo and Juliet feel for each other that takes over their lives and leads them into a marriage that goes against the traditions or beliefs of their respective families, namely, the Montagues and Capulets."

"Mighty big words the kiss-ass Jew boy uses!" somebody muttered behind Manuel, who turned around and frowned at the prejudiced freshman.

Manuel figured that, if the bigoted guy who had just made the ethnic statement hated Mike Bloom, an American-born student but a religious minority at Central Catholic High School, then the asshole would probably hate Manuel as well. After all, wasn't Manuel an ethnic minority (in terms of his mother language) and, on top of that, a recent immigrant?

"Excellent," Mr. Devlin said with an encouraging smile. "So the first union, through matrimony, constitutes an affront against the society they live in. And their final union, through mutual suicide, is an affront against what?"

"Against their Catholic faith!" John cried out, a slight note of irritation in his voice, his fat cheeks glowing rosier than usual.

"That's right," Mr. Devlin said.

"But you said libido was a life force," Manuel argued. "By the end of the last act, though, there are dead bodies lying all over the place. So isn't this libido more like a destructive thing than a life force?"

"Excellent observation, Mr. Cruz. Love is both life and death. Every birth, every life, carries the seed of death, and with every death there is a rebirth. After the deaths of Romeo and Juliet, as well as those of Mercutio, Tybalt, and Paris, the Capulets and Montagues end their senseless feud and are reborn to love. So life is death, and death is rebirth, and love encompasses all."

When Devlin entered a discussion of this sort, he would suddenly turn, it seemed to Manuel, into a walking energy storm, his blue eyes flashing like lightning, his voice bursting from the pit of his stomach with great force and echoing inside the classroom like thunder. He would pace up and down from one side of the classroom to the other in front of the class, not in a straight line but more in the pattern of an ellipse traced around the teacher's desk.

"The brain-storming egg walk" he had called it on the second day of class.

In his orbit-like pacing, as he would approach the blackboard, he would often seize the opportunity to make on it with a piece of yellow chalk all kinds of slashes that would end up being circles and Xs and wiggly and curved lines representing ideas and concepts. He preferred to use yellow-colored chalk, he had once explained, to underscore the notion life should not be seen in terms of only black and white. An English word or caption would never be written on the blackboard in association to the symbolic abstractions he would quickly scribble there, the students thus being forced to pay riveting attention to Mr. Devlin's "peripatetic lecture", as he had dubbed it. If at any time they lost the convoluted thread of his lecture, they were bound to get hopelessly lost in his maze of strange, wild ideas.

"Socrates didn't have the luxury of a blackboard," he had reminded his nine-grade students on an occasion. "Furthermore, his disciples didn't even have pens or pencils or notebooks or even desks to sit at and write on. They'd sit on top of big rocks out in the open, hopefully under a tree to get a little shade. So why should I write words up on the blackboard and make things insultingly easy for you guys? Symbols will do. Just listen well and let the ideas sink in and carve themselves into your soul forever."

Although the symbolic meaning of each primitive sign Mr. Devlin drew on the board changed constantly on a daily basis, one particular mark, however, stayed constant in that regard: the circle. This was always linked to the idea of womanhood or love or eternity.

John raised a thick arm. "Are you saying suicide is good?"

"No, I'm not. I'm saying it's neither good nor bad," Mr. Devlin said, as he continued to pace like a panther packed with megawatts of electricity about to explode and electroshock everybody in the room. "I'm saying it's beyond good and evil," he asserted, glaring fiercely in a way that challenged the class to contradict him.

"But the Church says it's bad," John whined.

"What Church?"

"The Catholic Church."

"And what's the Catholic Church?"

There was a long silence.

"A religion," said Frank timidly.

"And what's a religion?"

Another silence fell on the class.

"Think. What's the original meaning of religion?"

The silence thickened.

"Alright, I'll enlighten you. It comes from the Latin word 'religare', which signifies 'to link back'. Could anyone tell me what religion links back to?"

Elias, a tall, brawny student of Lebanese descent with kinky short-cropped hair and mulatto facial features, answered: "Religion links us back to God."

"And who is God?"

"The First Mover," said Rick Stramondo, whom some students called Pencil because of his sharply pointed head.

The theological concept had been freshly learned that morning in religion class, and Mike Bloom and Manuel rolled their eyes at each other and exchanged smirks.

"Real original," Mike whispered to his friend through the side of his mouth.

"And who's that?" Mr. Devlin asked.

"The guy upstairs," Rick said, pointing a finger toward the ceiling.

"Upstairs? He could be down that way, too. After all, isn't the world round and in the middle of space? Thus, He could also be that way." Mr. Devlin extended an arm to his right. "Or that way." He extended his other to the left, without dropping the first arm and, thus, leaving himself looking like a human cross. "Or... or...," he said, sliding his way over to where Richard was sitting, "*this way!*" And he poked a finger smack into the center of the freshman's chest.

Rick collapsed onto the back support of the chair.

"That's where God is. That's where Christ is. You know who Christ was?" Again he started pacing from side to side like a hounded animal, or a madman. "He was a human being, just like you and I, only he was lucky enough to experience the divinity of his own existence and to become, by so doing, a god. And how did he attain this experience? By descending into his inner being and reaching that core which is in everyone and links every person to every other human being, dead, alive, or yet to be born, that has walked, walks, or will walk the earth, that core or inner radiance which makes existence whole and is, in essence, the Christhood. You and you and you can become a Christ," he asserted, directing the tip of the extended index finger of his right hand like the muzzle of a gun. "*I* can become a Christ. *We all,*" he said, drawing loops with his index finger in midair, "*can become Christ.*"

Suddenly, the bell rang, but quite a number of students remained glued to their seats, as if stone-deaf to the loud ringing sound.

Manuel had been left breathless and at the same time unsatisfied. He felt Devlin had failed to explain fully one thing: why suicide was beyond good and evil.

Chapter X

"Hmm. So you seem to admire this, ah, Meester Devleen very, very much."

"Mister Devlin," Manuel said, amending her pronunciation.

Madama Farfalla tried to say the teacher's name again but mispronounced it once more, putting the stress on the final syllable and turning the last vowel sound into a long "e".

"You talk about him often," she said with a soft smile, "and when you do, your eyes light up."

"He's by far the most talked-about teacher in the school," Manuel commented. "But, of course, that's because he's an exceptionally eccentric person. He makes you think but also leaves you puzzled."

As Madama Farfalla's eyes slowly dropped their gaze toward her coffee cup, the smile wilted on her face.

Catching the sudden mood shift, he said: "You know, I've talked to him about you *a lot*, too."

She emitted a little gasp. "You talk to him about *me?*" she said, placing the palm of a hand flat against her chest, the long, supple fingers giving the impression of being perfectly made instruments for playing the piano despite her age. "You talk to him about old Madama Farfalla?"

"Why not?"

"*Tu non mi menti?*"

"Of course not. I'd never lie to you," he said. "Why should I? I even told him I had taken Italian at school because of you. Howdda you like that?" he added, knowing quite well that the main motivation for his choosing Italian as a freshman elective had been his desire to read Dante's *Divine Comedy* in the original language as much as he could. So far, however, the learning of the language was proving to be more useful to him in understanding the opera records Madama Farfalla periodically gave him as gifts as well as the phrases and sentences in Italian the old woman sprinkled her speech with than in cracking the masterpiece's abstruse medieval language.

"What did you tell this Mister Devleen about me?" she asked, her eyes opening very wide like those of a curious child.

"I told him you were once an opera singer."

"*Una diva. Una prima donna,*" she corrected with overflowing pride. "You tell him that?"

"Well, I'm afraid I failed to use those specific terms. So forgive me. I'll tell him next time. All the same, he was very much impressed with the fact you had sung operas professionally."

"You tell him I sing the part of Cio-Cio San in *Madame Butterfly*?" she questioned with burning black eyes.

"Ah, yes. I did, I did, as a matter of fact," Manuel stammered. "And he replied he had seen the opera at the Metropolitan Opera House."

"And you tell him I play the role of Violetta in *La Traviata*?"

Manuel paused to think for a moment, growing a bit suspicious. Had she thrown out this last bit of operatic autobiography like bait on a hook to catch him at work on a white lie?

"You never told me you had sung in *La Traviata*," he challenged.

Her breath sounded as if it had gotten caught on a thorn in her throat, and she automatically raised a hand to her mouth. "I never tell you?"

"Never."

"Oh, I'm sorry," she said with an almost imperceptible smile, and raised her coffee cup to her wrinkled lips, where now and again flickered the shadow of a vanished sensuality.

"What's the opera about?"

Manuel had already heard the synopsis of the opera from his older brother but didn't mind hearing Madama Farfalla retell the story.

She stared at him over the coffee cup, her lips frozen over its edge. "It's a silly old opera. Nothing much to it," she said peremptorily, dropping the cup on the saucer with a forceful clank. "You would not like it." She paused, and then, managing a half-hearted smile, said, "So, you were saying about Meester Devleen..."

"Oh, of course," Manuel said, quite happy to get back to one of his favorite topics of conversation as long as the topic didn't make Madama Farfalla feel uncomfortable. "Sometimes I just don't know where he gets the courage to say some of the things he does. He could easily get fired for it. After all, he does teach at a *Catholic* school."

"*Che cosa ha detto, per esempio?*"

"Oh, the other day he started discussing the use of mythology in Shakespeare."

He saw her furrow her eyebrows.

"Ah, mythology—how would you say that in Italian? *Mitologia?*" Manuel said

"Ah, *mitologia, si,*" she replied.

"Well, he said Shakespeare used references to mythological gods and goddesses to raise to a higher or divine level what the characters were supposed to be experiencing. You follow me?" he asked, and took a sip from his espresso.

Madama Farfalla nodded her head, saying, "*Capisco.*"

"Especially when what they were experiencing was love. Then he said Shakespeare, although a Christian, used these pagan mythological figures precisely because Christianity lacked such emotional wealth. The goddess, in particular, he said, had been wiped out of Christian thinking, except perhaps for the Catholic cult of the Virgin Mary, who wasn't really considered a goddess by the Church."

Madama Farfalla raised a hand in the way people do when they take an oath. "Just before my husband dies, I call *un sacerdote*, a priest, to come administer the last rites to my husband, who is suffering from this disease I call *vecchiaia*, old age. Others call it Alzheimer's." Her eyes wrinkled in a sad smile. "My husband—he loses his memory and becomes a vegetable more and more each day. He talks deliriously in bed and confuses me with other people. He begins to say he wants to be put in a nursing home. I tell him a nursing home is no good, old people are treated very badly there. He does not listen. We argue foolishly. All the time he gets worse and worse. He falls into a coma. So I say to myself, 'Madama Farfalla, it is time to call *il sacerdote!*' I do this because my husband is very religious. *Il prete* comes and I let him into that bedroom," she said, pointing with her head toward the room, now perfectly silent, where she played her opera records, sometimes at full blast. "I sit here in the kitchen and wait. When the priest finishes, he comes to me and says, 'Can I ask you a question?' '*Si, Padre,*' I say. He says, 'Why don't I ever see you in church?' For a minute my mind goes blank and I can say *nulla*, but then something comes to my head and I say, '*Padre*, the last time I was in church was in *Tosca*, but that was not a true church, you understand. It is a stage scene, where I play Floria Tosca. But with all due *rispetto*, Padre, I say this much: I will go back to a real church the day I can see a woman *sacerdote* say mass at the altar."'

Manuel opened his eyes very wide with a mixture of astonishment and admiration. Then suddenly he started laughing, spitting coffee on his sweaty woolen shirt.

She smiled and looked very pleased and enthused with the youth's reaction. "*Il prete* gets up right away and with a very angry face makes the sign of the cross at me like I am Dracula or the devil or a *witcha* and runs out of the apartment. Maybe he is the person who tells the neighborhood *bambini* I am a *witcha*."

She joined his chuckling, being careful to cover her mouth. "You like the story, huh?"

"It was great!" Manuel said, still laughing. "Mr. Devlin would love it!" he blurted out, holding his sides. Regaining control of himself, he went on to say, "That reminds me of something. You know what Mr. Devlin did one day? I didn't witness this, but somebody who has him first period described to me in detail what had happened, and then later on another student confirmed the story. Well, one morning Brother Marcel, the school disciplinarian, overslept or something and didn't make it on time or simply forgot to say the morning prayers over the PA system. So Mr. Devlin said he was going to lead the morning prayers instead of the absent Marist brother for his first period class. He began by making the sign of the cross and saying, 'In the name of the Mother and of the Son and of the Holy Ghost, Amen.' The students were in shock. Then, to make things worse, he said, 'Let's say an "Our Mother".' And he went on to recite the weirdest Our Father. It supposedly went something like this: 'Our Mother, who art in heaven, hallowed be thy name...' God! All the students were freaking out! They could hardly believe their ears. Well, this fat kid nicknamed Porky hit the roof right away when he heard about it, crying it was heresy to mess around with the Lord's Prayer. So he brought up the issue later that day in our English class with Devlin. Very calmly, Mr. Devlin replied he hadn't been playing or even kidding one bit, that, in fact, he had been dead serious. 'After all,' he explained, 'only a woman can give birth and create life. So, if God is the source of all life, then God must be a She, which is to say, a Woman and a Mother.' Crazy, huh?"

Madama Farfalla sighed deeply and tried to pick up her cup, but her trembling hand fumbled with it. She set it down and released it, perhaps to avoid spilling some of its content.

Manuel saw a tear had welled up in one of her big dark eyes.

"Did I say something wrong?" he asked, afraid he might have offended her religious sensibilities as Mr. Devlin had done to John, alias Porky, a religious fanatic.

She shook her head and wiped away the tear with a couple of limber fingers, suddenly giving Manuel the impression that, when an old woman cried, in some strange way she came across as an ageless person, a single human tear being capable of washing away the oldest birthday records.

"It is just that lately I get very sentimental over little things," she said. Her voice trailed off, coming close to ending in a sob.

Manuel remained silent. He intuited that deep down inside she had an aching need to reveal something but was reluctant or afraid to do so.

She labored to her feet and took their cups.

"Do you want more coffee?" she asked haltingly.

"Yes," Manuel said, although he distinctly remembered that his mother had told him to curtail his visitation time to Madama Farfalla's dark, tomb-like apartment and, furthermore, to accept nothing offered by the strange Italian lady to drink or eat. Maria feared the worst: that the old hag was a sorceress, *una bruja*, a witch of some sort, who was trying to ensnare an innocent young boy like Manuel for who knew what purposes. In Cuba there had been women, Maria had pointed out, who cast spells on young men and adolescents through strange love potions.

Madama Farfalla filled his cup as well as hers with more coffee and trudged back to the table, holding both cups. Because of the tremor in her hands, some of the coffee was spilled on the linoleum floor but she didn't seem to notice this, so distantly her mind had wandered off.

"As a little girl, I play with dolls and always pretend I was the mother of the dolls," she began, and blew air rapidly through her nose as if she were about to break into chuckles. No sounds of laughter, however, came from her; neither did the smallest smile surface on her lips.

Another tear, though, did manage to get squeezed from an eye, but she did not bother to wipe the tear away this time and went on with her story.

By the time she met her future husband, she was a rising opera star, singing all over *Italia*. She was only one small step away from performing in La Scala in Milano. Soon after she got married, she told tell her husband, "A child is much more important to me than a thousand appearances at La Scala."

They tried hard to have a child. But *nulla*. Nothing. No luck.

They went to see doctors everywhere. They all would tell the newlywed couple to try this, to try that. *Nothing*. No results. One day they went to see a famous gypsy woman, who told Madama Farfalla her future. She would die a beautiful death, like one of the characters she would play.

"We didn't come here to have you tell us *il futuro della mia moglie*," Madama Farfalla's husband the barber complained. "We came here to have you tell us what we must do to have a baby."

The gypsy gave the husband an icy look and then said, "She will have a son, not of the body, but of the spirit."

Madama Farfalla's husband got very mad and called her *una ciarlatana*. Then he got up and pulled Madama Farfalla by the arm and made her leave immediately without letting her drop a tip in a big glass jar near the front door of the gypsy woman's house.

"Charlatans do not deserve a tip," he growled outside.

Just the same, Madama Farfalla came back the next day and gave the gypsy lady some *liras*. Madama Farfalla asked her about what she had said the day before, and she merely slammed the front door in the singer's face, but only after taking the money.

Then one night after a performance of *Madame Butterfly* in Napoli, her birthplace, Madama Farfalla told her husband she wanted to do something *folle*, something crazy.

It was raining.

"Rain is life," she told him. "It makes things grow, like trees and crops. Rain is love. It is the seed of heaven. It makes flowers bloom, rivers flow. It fills the oceans. So maybe, if it is good for Mother Earth, it is good for me, too. Maybe it will make my belly get big with life and love. Let's take a walk in the rain and I will sing to you *canzoni d'amore napoletane.*'

"Do I have to get wet, too?" her husband asked, scared like a child.

"No," Madama Farfalla answered. "You just come along with your umbrella and listen to me sing Neapolitan love songs."

It was raining cats and dogs. Madama Farfalla got drenched. Her husband tried to cover himself with the umbrella but still got his feet very wet. He caught pneumonia. His wife caught cold. So in her first appearance ever at La Scala as Cio-Cio San, Madama Farfalla sang with a serious sore throat, while her husband stayed in the hospital. It was better that he hadn't gone as the spectators booed his wife off the stage that night.

Madama Farfalla paused in her narration, her face, like an evening moon, quickly losing its glow behind a dark, ominous passing cloud.

"Then I develop an infection in the left ear and start having problems hearing. I stop singing and I never get to perform again at La Scala and prove to the Milanese opera lovers I am one of the best singers to play Cio-Cio San ever," she said, sighing deeply.

Manuel felt paralyzed and alarmed simultaneously at the poignant intensity of the moment. Tears had welled up again in Madama Farfalla's eyes. But some voice inside told him that at the present time he could not just simply get up and, under some lame excuse, make an exit as if nothing had happened. Given the highly emotional state of Madama Farfalla, such an action on his part might have the same effect on her as a stake driven into her heart or a viper's poison injected into her blood system.

He decided a quick change of subject would be the best antidote for her worsening depression.

"Did I tell you I went to see a rerun of *West Side Story*?"

She shook her head, the tears squirming down her cheeks. Despite her advanced age, she looked girlish when she swayed her head and made her hair copious hair, profusely sprinkled with grey, flop from side to side.

"Well, you see, Mr. Devlin had told the class that a movie theater in Andover was playing *West Side Story*, which was, he said, a modern version of the Romeo-and-Juliet plot. He encouraged his students to go see it. Frank Scuito, a classmate of mine at Central, and I decided to go see it together, and he invited a couple of freshman girls from St. Mary's High School to come along with us. His mother drove us there, and we had a fine time. But I would have had a much better time if the St. Mary's freshman named Peggy Thomas had allowed me to hold her hand during the movie," he said, and smiled, hoping such a remark would humor the old soprano a bit and aid her in forgetting her troubled past, at least for the moment. "She played hard to get on me, though, saying we had just met and I was going too fast and all that baloney."

Madama Farfalla, who, while Manuel had been speaking, had dabbed away at the wet spots on her face with a red handkerchief magically produced out of somewhere inside her ample black dress, presently made with the hanky the playful gesture of wanting to throw it at him.

"You *cascamorto*," she said, feigning irritation.

"*Cascamorto?*"

"Yes, *cascamorto*. A flirt," she revealed.

"Oh," Manuel said, chuckling.

Then, squeezing the handkerchief with both her hands against her bosom and rolling her eyes upward, the former prima donna cried in anguish: "Romeo, oh, Romeo, *dove stai, che non ti vedo*, oh, *infedele* Romeo?"

Manuel burst out in laughter, exaggerating it a bit to make sure Madama Farfalla became aware that he appreciated her histrionics. In truth, he felt happy witnessing such good-natured playacting, which reflected a sudden change of mood on the former diva's part.

Her laughter shortly joined his, gushing forth like a jet of fresh water out of a revived old well. Soon she was laughing so hard, tears of joy splashed her cheeks. But although she seemed to surrender completely to the hilarity of the moment, at no time did she forget to shield her mouth with her red hankie.

Chapter XI

"What kind of music is that?"

Manuel was lying on the sofa with his feet up, reading Charles Dickens' *Great Expectations* in a leisurely way while listening to a record. Before answering his mother, he lowered the thick novel to his lap and perked up his ears. Had he just heard the barking of the neighborhood dogs? It was barking alright, but it came from too great a distance to signal the arrival of the mailman on the block.

"*Orfeo ed Euridice* by Gluck," he answered his mother. "It's a symphonic opera. Madama Farfalla gave it to me as a gift."

Maria shook her head disapprovingly, while continuing to knit away at what was supposed to end up as a sweater for her younger son Esteban several months from now.

"More opera records? Don't you get tired of listening to them? More gifts? Is there no end to them? That music seems to get worse all the time. This record, in particular, sounds like something you'd hear from a choir at a church funeral."

Manuel smiled. "Do you know the story of Orpheus and Eurydice?"

"No, I'm afraid not," she replied without peeling her eyes off her manual work for even a split second. "I wasn't as lucky as you to have gone to high school or get opera records from a former singer."

Manuel frowned but went on to say: "Orpheus was a Greek hero, the son of one of the Muses. He was known for the beauty of his singing voice and his skill with the lyre. When he made music, rivers would change their courses and stones would move and form a circle around him."

"That can't be true," Maria complained categorically, undoing a couple of stitches.

"And what is truth?" Manuel said, ready for philosophical debate with his mother, although he wasn't sure of how well she would take it. She wasn't usually very tolerant or open-minded when she argued. Noticing that she made no attempt to answer his question, he went on to observe: "Sure, the story is a myth, but it's a beautiful one."

As Maria continued to knit, he told her the story of Orpheus and Eurydice.

Orpheus fell in love with this young lady called Eurydice, but on their wedding day the new bride stepped on a viper. Stung by it, she died. Orpheus loved Eurydice so much he decided to descend into the underworld and persuade the gods down there to release his young wife. He charmed them with his lyre and voice and they agreed to let her go on one condition—that he not look at her until both he and Eurydice had emerged from the cavern of death. Well, he made precisely that fatal mistake, glancing back at Eurydice just before she had had a chance to come out fully onto the light of life, and she fell back into the netherworld and was lost to him forever.

Maria shook her head, frowning. "That's a very depressing story. Is that the only type of records this old woman gives you?"

"Not really. She gave me this set of records because I mentioned the story to her," Manuel argued. "You see, Mr. Devlin, my English teacher, brought up in class the other day the notion Romeo was an Orpheus-like figure. Well, I mentioned this to her, and she said that there was an opera based on the Greek story and she'd get it for me. And that's what happened."

"So you can discuss such things with that witch downstairs but not with me, your very own mother, huh? And what does that mumbo-jumbo about Romeo and what's-his-name mean?"

"It means Romeo and Orpheus resemble each other in certain things. For example, they are both young newlyweds when their respective spouses die. Juliet drinks a potion that puts her into a death-like sleep and is buried in a tomb, while Eurydice suffers a snake bite, dies from the viper's venom, a sort of animal potion, you could say, and is sent to the gloomy underworld. Romeo goes down into Juliet's tomb, a kind of underworld in itself, and, thinking she's truly dead, commits suicide. When Juliet wakes up and finds her husband dead, she stabs herself, thus suffering a second death in a way. Orpheus, in turn, goes down into the actual underworld and almost rescues his wife from the jaws of death, only he forgets his agreement with the gods and looks at his wife, bringing upon her a second death as she's swallowed up again into the dark abyss."

"*Dios mío,* some big words my son is learning at that Marist school! Pretty soon I'm going to need a dictionary and an encyclopedia to understand him!"

"I wrote a paper on the Romeo-Orpheus parallelism for Mr. Devlin's English class and got an A."

"And I'm sure you ran to the old Italian lady with the news and she gave you a peck on the cheek."

Manuel shook his head with deep sadness without making any comment.

Maria yawned prodigiously, as if she were in need of a Saturday afternoon siesta. Then she said: "I hope one day soon you stop seeing that crazy old woman. She truly gives me the creeps, I swear, with those black dresses of hers and that eerie music she plays and that apartment she keeps so dark and musty."

"You're making a mountain out of molehill," Manuel replied. "Actually, she's a very down-to-earth person and has got a very good hold of all her senses. Besides, she's very kind and generous and sweet. Anyway, no matter how you look at it, you can't deny she's a paper-route customer of mine and I must deliver the paper to her door."

"But, as a paper boy, you don't have to go inside her apartment and have little chitchats with her so often. *Or do you?* All you're expected to do is deliver the paper, period. That place of hers is as dark as a cave or a grave. It's never ventilated, I'm sure. The darkest, stuffiest church would look like a greenhouse on a sunny summer day in comparison to that gloomy place of hers shut off from the world for I don't know what reason. What does she have in there anyway? A secret witch's altar dedicated to the devil or something? Maybe she's a Satanist."

"Come on, *Mami*. Don't exaggerate like that! It's not nice," Manuel said, picking up his book. "In reality, as I've said, you're creating a storm in a teacup."

"How about in a *coffee cup?*" she said with a sarcastic smile.

Explosive voices, coming out of Juan and Pablo's bedroom, reached the living room like a small tidal wave.

"Oh, Jesus, they're going at it again," Manuel grunted.

"Yes, they've been bickering on and off most of the day," Maria commented, putting on her lap her knitting implements and yarns. "When you were doing your paper route, it got really nasty, and I shut myself up in my room. I'm starting to worry. Since Pablo totaled the car and neither of them has a personal means of transportation, they've had to stay in the apartment and see more of each other whether they like it or not. So their quarrels have become more frequent and louder."

Manuel sat up straight on the sofa and slipped the Dickens' book onto the small end table.

"Juan can be kind of violent, you know," Manuel said. "Maybe he and Pablo ought to split up or something. What I mean is maybe Pablo should move out."

"That's really none of our business, Manuel," Maria scolded. "We should not interfere in private quarrels, unless our opinion is asked. Even then we should keep our opinion to ourselves."

"Things could get pretty ugly and mean between those two," Manuel insisted, "especially if Juan loses his cool. He's like a time bomb. You know what he once told me? That he had almost killed somebody back in Cuba!"

"I can't believe that!" she said, laying aside her knitting paraphernalia on the end table near the recliner where she was sitting. "Juan wouldn't hurt a fly. He even studied to be a priest."

"Juan was the one who told me he almost killed someone one day back in Cuba. He even told me who it was he almost killed—*intentionally!*"

"Oh, my God, who?"

"My father's mistress."

She looked into her son's eyes fixedly for some time and then, lifting her gaze, said in a whispery voice, "How unfortunate he failed!"

"Juan said he tried to kill her after seeing *La Traviata?*"

"*La Traviata?*"

"It's an opera about a former prostitute."

Maria moved her head back a little and laughed softly. "Don't you get it?"

"No. Not really."

"Your father's mistress at one time plied the world's oldest profession, too. Well, I should correct myself. She was, is, and always will be a *prostitute* at heart," she said with venomous relish. "Once a whore, always a whore."

"Did my father meet her when she was a lady of the evening?"

"A lady of the evening? How poetic! You mean a whore working at a *burdel*."

"What's that?"

"*Una casa de putas*. A whore house. Please pardon my language."

"She worked in one of those places?" Manuel said, falling back against the couch in pure shock.

"And for several years."

"So she was like Violetta in *La Traviata*," he concluded.

Maria paid no attention to her son's comparison and went on with her story about her husband's lover.

The place was called Marta y Belona, famous in Havana, a mixture of nightclub and brothel. Men could go there, listen to music, order drinks and food, and ask any of the ladies who worked there to dance with them. If a man liked what fell into his arms, he could request a room upstairs and so forth.

"The joint was famous," Maria insisted. "So Manolo's *puta* must have allowed armies of men, of every nationality, color, shape, and size, do whatever they wished on her."

Manuel blushed, not liking the graphic way his mother was relating certain circumstances concerning his father's paramour's life.

"That's the kind of human garbage your father prefers over me," she suddenly said in a sharp voice, rising to her feet.

As she stomped out of the living room, a door slammed somewhere inside the apartment, startling Manuel.

"What was that?" he asked his mom.

Maria didn't look back, frozen in her steps.

"Juan, what's wrong?" he then heard her say.

"Nothing." It was Juan's voice. "Everything is fine with me. He's the one who's got a problem, a *mental* one. But I'm not going to let that ruin my life. He can destroy all the cars he wants. But he's not going to destroy me."

"Where are you going?" Maria asked in a strained voice.

"I'll be by the river. I need to cool off. I don't want to do something I'll later..."

Juan darted through the living room and out the front door so quickly, he did not even notice Manuel's presence there. He was breathing heavily and carried a set of binoculars in his hand.

Maria rushed into the parlor. "Manuel, why don't you follow him? He's liable to do something crazy."

"Relax. He's not going to drown himself in the Lawrence River," Manuel retorted. "I don't think it's deep enough for starters."

"But he can be violent. You said so yourself."

"Only with someone he's angry at and it so happens that *that someone* is locked up in the bedroom over there," Manuel said, pointing with his chin. "So he's better off putting distance between himself and that bedroom. Besides, he's definitely not going to kill any river birds with his binoculars."

Maria made a face. "Still, I'd feel much better if you kept an eye on him while I talk to poor Pablo. Just be with your brother for a while, will you please?"

"Alright," Manuel said a bit reluctantly. "It's silly and unnecessary, but if it'll make you feel better..." Then he heard the awaited barking from the neighborhood dogs. "That's the mailman!" he cried with alacrity. "I'm expecting my report card!"

He flew down the stairs at break-neck speed, skipping two steps at a time.

"How ya doing, young cat?" said the black mailman. "You looking good, you looking good. Getting bigger all the time, huh?"

"Yeah. Got something for me?"

"Sure, baby," the mailman replied with a big grin, and handed him a single envelope.

Manuel glanced at the return address and said, "Thanks."

It was exactly what he had been waiting for. He strutted out into the autumn sun and ripped the envelope open as he walked down the sidewalk in the direction of the public school by the Lawrence River.

It was the first time his eyes perused a marking-period report card from Central Catholic, but his mind easily managed to decipher the most crucial information he anxiously sought. In a class of 212 freshmen, he ranked fifth for the first marking period. Wow! That was neat! It meant he had won a marking-period scholarship! He started leaping up and down, clicking his heels in midair, right smack in the middle of the street as he crossed it.

"Hey, young cat, what you so happy about?" shouted the mailman.

"I just won a scholarship on my own!"

"I guess writing so many letters to a gallant lady improves the mind after all," the mailman said, smiling and winking an eye at Manuel. "Just don't get run over by a truck now, ya hear?"

Manuel started running toward the Lawrence River, a tributary to the Merrimack River, which ran wide, deep, and majestic through the heart of the factory section in Lawrence. He galloped across the schoolyard, sneaked through a large gaping hole in a wire fence, and stepped, out of breath, onto a grassy bank where a dried-out fountain stood.

Juan was sitting against a tree, looking across the stream with his binoculars.

"I won a scholarship!" Manuel cried at him.

Manuel hoped this pronouncement would not shatter the idyllic magic Juan seemed to find in this secret refuge.

"I thought you already had one," Juan said quite calmly, as he continued to scour the trees on the opposite bank in their glorious display of autumnal colors.

"No, that was different. That was an act of generosity from some secret benefactor," Manuel explained. "This marking-period scholarship is something *I earned*," he stated, proudly slapping his chest like a scholastic Tarzan. "I came in fifth out of 212 freshmen this marking period. The top-five ranked students each marking period get a scholarship to be used the following period."

Juan lowered his field glasses. "Congratulations," he said, forcing a grin, and stuck out his hand, which his younger brother shook. A long silence followed, broken by an apology. "Sorry about the outburst back there."

"Gee, I didn't hear a thing," Manuel said.

"Have a seat," Juan offered, pointing at the grass littered with dry fallen leaves. "But if your schooling is all paid for by some anonymous person, what's the sense of getting a scholarship like that?"

"That's precisely what I was discussing with Madama Farfalla the other day," Manuel replied, "after I started seeing the possibility of my coming in among the top five this marking period. Well, she suggested I go talk to an administrator at Central Catholic and demand the scholarship be paid directly to me in cash. I could use it, she said, to buy books to build up a personal library and to buy LPs for my collection of opera records. What do you think of her idea?"

"Not a bad one," Juan commented, and then let his eyes drift down the river and its gentle current. After a while, he said: "By the way, Manuel, I'm getting married next summer."

"You're joshing! Well, gee, congratulations to you, too!"

The two brothers shook hands again. "Who's the lucky girl?"

"A local girl."

"Cuban?"

"French-Canadian."

"*Parlez-vous francais, monsieur?*" Manuel said with a smile.

The first person to teach him French had been Sister Imelda, who was from the province of Quebec, and that had been the first French phrase he had learned with her. Now he was taking French at Central Catholic High School from a Marist Brother who was also a Canadian native and was reputed to be a fairy. Manuel didn't know whether that was true or not. But the gray-haired middle-aged man sure loved to caress the students around the thighs while they sat doing class exercises at their desks.

"*Seulement un peu,*" Juan answered, and chuckled.

"You're going to have a big wedding?"

"Not at all. She and I are just going to go to city hall and get married there through a notary public."

"No church wedding?"

"Maybe later. Who knows? The important thing is being joined in marriage."

Manuel noticed right away that Juan had failed to use the adjective "holy" before the word "marriage".

"Gee, that doesn't sound like you, Juan."

"Maybe."

"I guess she's not Catholic, huh? Although most French-Canadians are, I would guess."

"How did you know?" Juan queried, looking surprised.

"It makes sense. You're not getting married in the Church and you didn't say *holy* marriage."

Juan laughed and slapped my shoulder. "You're a

smart cookie, aren't you? Yeah, you're right. She's not Catholic. She's Jewish."

"Oh, my God, that's really something!" Manuel chuckled. "Wait till I tell my friend Mike Bloom about it!"

"Who's he?"

"A Jewish friend of mine."

"Ah, I see. Anyway, I'm sure we'll be a happy couple. That's what counts. The rest is bullshit," Juan said through the side of his mouth.

"What made you, if I may ask, want to tie the knot so... uh... suddenly?"

Juan pulled up a few fallen leaves from the ground and tossed them at the stream. A gentle cool breeze caught them and made them fall back on his legs.

"*Un pajarito!*" he suddenly whispered.

"Did I hear you right? Did you say 'a little bird'?" Manuel said, examining Juan's face closely to make sure his brother wasn't playing a joke on him.

"That's right," Juan replied, a very serious expression on his countenance. "As you know, my mother died when I was a youngster, and ever since I've always had the feeling that she didn't really leave me but stayed around to watch, protect, and guide me." He threw a small stone into the Lawrence River and then went on to say: "Well, one day when I was sitting on a bench in Caibarien's central park, pondering over whether I should leave Cuba or not, I heard something or someone whistle in the exact same way my mother used to do when she wanted to call me as a kid to come home. I immediately turned around and saw the most beautiful cardinal I'd ever laid eyes on. It was perched on a tree bough right behind me. Suddenly, it flew toward me and started flapping its wings over my head, like it wanted to tell me something, you know what I mean?"

Manuel nodded although he found Juan's story a bit hard to swallow.

Juan said that right then and there he had remembered what his mom had once told me when she had been bed-ridden with cancer.

"Don't you worry about me, son," she had told him. "After I'm gone, I'll come back as a bird and whisper things in your ear so that you know I'm near."

With the appearance of the cardinal, he had felt a strong charge of electricity run up and down his spine. Shortly afterwards, he had distinctly heard the bird hum something like, "Go, Go. Get out of Cuba." He had interpreted this as a message from his dead mom telling him to leave the island—which he did.

Juan went on to say he had seen another special bird about a month before right there by the river while he had sat where he was at that very moment. He pointed with an arm to his right at a ruined concrete structure that looked like the remnant of an old wall by the edge of the water. He had heard the same whistling and witnessed the same flapping of wings around his head when the bird had flown in his direction, and he had experienced the same explosion of electricity up and down his spinal cord. Then the same humming voice had spoken to him. The only difference had been that the bird which had appeared to him by the crumbling wall had been a goldfinch instead of a cardinal.

He paused in his story and swallowed hard, his eyes filming over. "And I swear to you over my mother's grave," he said, making a cross with his fingers and kissing the middle of it, "that I heard the critter whisper to me: 'Do it! Do it! Go on and get married!'"

With grave concern Manuel looked at Juan, who was wiping away the tears with the back of a hand.

"I didn't think you believed in such things," Manuel said, befuddled.

"To tell the truth, I don't know anymore what to believe in," Juan confessed with a sigh. "By the way, Simone— that's my fiancée's name—Simone and I will be moving to New Hampshire once we get married. We hope to find peace and quiet up there in the New Hampshire woods away from the hustle and bustle of city life."

"New Hampshire is a nice state," Manuel mumbled, although a certain fear started gnawing inside of him. "Mother Nature and stuff with beautiful autumns and gorgeous setting suns and all that." He sighed heavily. "But what about the apartment here? What about us? My mother, Esteban, myself?"

Juan patted him on the knee. "Relax. You've got nothing to worry about. The earth isn't going to swallow me up, you know. I'll come around to visit, and you, your mom, and little Esteban can come up to visit us, too. It's just that for a while I'm going to need some space to put things into perspective. Like everybody else, I'm in the process of trying to put myself together, if you know what I mean."

"I understand where you're coming from," Manuel said as if he really did.

"As far as the apartment is concerned," he continued, "you can go on living there as long as you and your mom wish to. I've already talked to the landlady, and she said she's very happy with you and your family and would be delighted to keep you all as tenants."

"And Pablo?" I asked nervously. "What about Pablo?"

"Oh, he'll have to move out and find himself a place somewhere else, that's all. Your mom told me that my father is sending her money now on a regular monthly basis and that she could afford the rent by herself. At any rate, one thing is for sure: you can always count on me to be there for you whenever you need me. I'll be only a phone's call away, my brother. Don't ever forget that."

"Thanks," Manuel said hoarsely, his fears somewhat assuaged for the moment. He rose to his feet. "Got to go," he added, brushing the small bits of grass and leaves off his blue jeans. "I want to give my mother the good news about the scholarship."

Juan waved a hand and picked up his field glasses again.

As Manuel opened the door to the apartment, anxious to tell his mother of his scholastic success, he heard heavy moans and groans coming from inside the house. With his heart racing, he stepped in.

There on the living room sofa, he saw Pablo sobbing away on Maria's shoulder. Manuel and his mother's eyes met, and he frowned and shook his head at her, sending out a clear message of disapproval with respect to what was happening. In truth, he felt sick to his stomach at the sight of a grown man crying like a little girl in front of a woman. In utter disgust, he turned his face away from the unmanly spectacle and walked briskly out of the living room and once again out of the apartment. As he did this, he could not help hearing a new torrent of lamentations.

"But I love him. I really do," Pablo wailed. "I love him so much. I can't go on living without him."

The sofa creaked from the sobs wracking his body.

"That's why I crashed the car against a tree. It was no accident. I did it on purpose! I did it intentionally *to kill myself*! But he cares more about the damn car than *about me*!"

Powerful sobbing once more filled the apartment.

A protective brotherly instinct brought the thought of Esteban to Manuel's mind. Where was the scrawny little kid? Manuel asked himself, frantically rushing back into the apartment and slipping into the bedroom Maria and Esteban shared. His little brother wasn't there and he felt deeply relieved to discover that.

Then he remembered having seen Esteban playing with some neighborhood kids outside the apartment as he had headed toward the Lawrence River to find Juan. It was indeed good that Esteban had been spared the wild effeminate drama put on by a grown man whose manly muscularity gave a different impression at first sight.

Manuel turned around and was about to shut the door of his mother's bedroom and enclose himself there in its privacy, when he heard more nerve-shattering groans.

"If he leaves me, I'll try to kill myself again! And this time *I won't fail*!

Chapter XII

A s he bathed, he belted out song after song, trying to imitate Mario Lanza's exuberant style. Several times his voice cracked as it climbed toward the high notes, but he felt no embarrassment with no one in the apartment except for Esteban, who was in the living room, enthralled by *The Flintstones* on television.

Afterwards, he went out and on Eden Street bought a bouquet of white camellias, which he wrapped in smooth glossy white paper. As he gingerly held the bouquet and took in its fragrance through flared nostrils, the Italian flower vendor asked: "Who are you buying these for, young man? Your mom? Or your girlfriend?" he said with a wink. "It's not Mother's Day, you know."

Manuel smiled at the humorous remark but didn't give an answer. Then he strode off, discreetly humming Lanza's *Be My Love*, a song that had captivated his fancy the moment he had heard it for the first time in Mrs. Di Giovanni's room at Manor Home.

As he began his walk toward the Holy Rosary convent, his mind began to wander away in reminiscences.

"That's a beautiful song!" Manuel had remarked, handing the newspaper to the tall lady with tinted blond hair.

"My boy Mario," Mrs. Di Giovanni said with pride, while carefully counting the coins out of her purse. She was always very exact with her week's payment, so much so that Manuel could not remember a single occasion when she had tipped him.

The day before Christmas, however, she had surprised him with a gift: a record album with Mario Lanza songs, which included *Be My Love*.

"That's so you can tell that old lady friend of yours— oh, what's her name?—that opera arias don't hold a monopoly on great love songs," Mrs. Di Giovanni said, waving a critical finger.

"You mean Madama Farfalla?"

"Yes, her. Maybe. Hmm, *strange*. I'd say I know most of, if not all, the Italian women who are old-timers in Lawrence, but her name doesn't seem to ring a bell. I did know someone, however, a former piano and voice teacher, who was addicted to operas, but her name definitely wasn't Farfalla. It was Giordano. Are you sure this woman's last name isn't Giordano?"

"I'm positive. It's Farfalla."

"Alright. Just the same, if you ever run into an old woman with the name Giordano," she said, holding her head up very straight like a woman of royal blood, "please let me know. She has a debt to pay me."

"You mean, she owes you money, Mrs. Di Giovanni?" Manuel said, remembering Rick, the former paperboy who owed him money the rascal had stolen from his route.

Mrs. Di Giovanni smiled gently. "No, no. Not that kind

of debt. She owes me in another way." She drew closer. "Have a very merry Christmas day tomorrow, my boy," she murmured and, bending her tall, regal frame, pecked him on the cheek.

So enraptured had he been by the Lanza songs that, when he had fallen in love, or rather had thought he had fallen in love, with Peggy Thomas, he had gone to a record shop and bought another *Be My Love* album and surprised her with it one Sunday after mass at Holy Rosary Church, hoping the record's musical romanticism would rub off on her as it had done on him.

Peggy had smiled embarrassedly. "Gee, thanks. It's got a beautiful cover. By the way, who's this Mario Lanza?" she suddenly asked, Anglicizing the pronunciation of the Italian name.

"He's a tenor, the greatest since Caruso."

"Is he Spanish?" she asked, the shadow of a doubt flitting across her face.

"Oh, no. He's a full-blooded American singer, born and raised in Philadelphia."

"But the music—is it rock-'n'-roll or what?" she quizzed, looking at him askance.

"Is that what you like? Rock-'n'-roll?"

"It's the only music I listen to," she said testily.

Her reply squeezed his heart. "Gee, I didn't know that. Oh, well, maybe next time I can get you a rock-'n'-roll record," he said dispiritedly.

A car horn sounded. "Well, I gotta go," she said with an artificial smile. "That's my dad. See you around."

"When can I see you again?" he asked in desperation.

"Pleeeze, whatever you do, don't wait for me after church again. My father doesn't like to see me talking to boys after mass. He says it's blasphemous." She glanced nervously over her shoulder. "What's worse, if he ever found out you went to the Spanish mass in the basement," she added in a whisper, "man, he'd grab me by the throat in a second and strangle me!"

Peggy's last comment knocked the breath out of Manuel. It had never occurred to him that the division of Holy Rosary Church into the spacious, well-lit, well-ventilated, classy upstairs church (for masses in English) and the church basement, converted into a gloomy, cramped, catacomb-like chapel (for masses for Spanish speakers), had put him at a disadvantage with the world at large by branding his forehead, so to speak, with some sort of mark like Cain's or relegating him to the "untouchables" caste.

"Well, I certainly wouldn't want to cause any problems between you and your dad," Manuel said humbly.

"I appreciate it," she said, and resumed her walk toward her dad's car, holding the LP record cover with just her fingertips as if at any time she might drop it into a garbage can.

"When will I see you again, Peggy?" he shouted even though he felt the situation was hopeless.

"I'll call you," she said curtly, without even looking back.

God, she had forgotten to thank him for the Mario Lanza LP! Well, maybe he could phone her that night and give her the chance to remember his gift and express her gratitude. But then he recalled she had also warned him about calling her at home. Her father, of Irish descent, had scolded her the last time Manuel had dialed her. Unfortunately, Peggy's dad had received the phone call, and he had later complained to her about a boy with a slight Spanish or Italian accent who had asked for his daughter.

That night he felt so depressed he phoned Frank Scuito and told his friend about his love problems.

Frank chuckled gently. "Don't you know she's going out with someone else?"

The news was not a major surprise to Manuel. Deep down inside he had suspected all along that she might be two-timing him. Still, the confirmation of his suspicion hurt badly.

"Anybody I know?"

"His name's Rick."

"Rick? Does he go to Central?"

"Oh, no. He's a public school boy," Frank said, "a junior at Lawrence High, although I've heard him brag he could have gone to Central with all expenses paid if he had really wanted. He said he had a woman friend who was willing to pay for his education at Central."

Manuel searched in his memory again but nothing registered.

"He says he knows you."

"From where?"

"The newspaper."

"The newspaper? Oh, you mean he's seen my picture in the *Eagle-Tribune* for winning the marking-period scholarships at Central Catholic?"

Manuel smiled at the thought that he was getting to be well-known on account of his high academic achievements.

"No, silly. Not from your picture in the paper. From your *paper route*."

"Oh, gosh, no! Not that bastard!" Manuel exploded, now making the right connection. "That scoundrel owes me money! He's a thief and an S.O.B.," he cried, letting the sharp words fly out of his mouth without any hesitation, for he felt fully justified in using them.

To confirm the startling information received that Sunday, Manuel decided to pass by St. Mary's High School the following day and observe the dismissal of the female student body there. St. Mary's High dismissed its students half an hour after most other area high schools did, giving Manuel plenty of time to set up his watch behind some vehicles in the school parking lot across the street from the school's main entrance. To make sure he got a good look at Rick, Manuel had taken his older brother's binoculars without asking for Juan's permission.

About two or three minutes before the dismissal bell sounded at the all-girls school, Rick showed up. He did not seem as big as when Manuel had met him some months back. But that was probably due, Manuel thought, to his having grown several quick inches in height since their last encounter on the paper route. Now he was probably about as tall as or taller than Rick.

After carefully putting away the field glasses in his school bag for safe keeping, Manuel crossed the parking lot and then the street.

Ten yards away from his rival, he called out: "Hey, Rick, remember me?"

Rick turned around slowly, in the way people who think they own a good portion of the world often do. On recognizing Manuel, he faked a smile.

"How you been, pal?" he said. His amiability sounded terribly phony. He then proffered a hand.

Manuel did not clasp it, after having determined Rick held no height advantage over him any longer.

"You owe me money," Manuel snarled, his voice quavering with anger, fueled by his memory of the paper-route swindle and his recent discovery of Peggy's disloyalty at the hands of his nemesis. "You owe me eleven dollars and fifteen cents, to be exact. That's how much you ripped me off for on that Friday when you took me for a joy ride on the route and got paid a week in advance from several of the customers without telling me about it."

"I think you've made a mistake, pal," he said, measuring Manuel's new physique, his Adam's apple going up and down. "Besides, I'm broke. I couldn't repay you even if I wanted to."

"Actually, I didn't really come to collect the debt in that manner," Manuel retorted ominously, and looked in the direction of the bevy of girls streaming out through the school's front gates.

"Now wait just one darn minute there, pal. Are you trying to pull something funny on me out here?" Rick said suspiciously, his face a mask of concern. When he saw Peggy, however, he flashed a big smile. "Hey, babe, what's happening?" he cried, trying to sound as happy and nonchalant as possible.

Peggy approached the two boys slowly, scowling at Manuel. "And what are *you* doing here, for heaven's sake?" she said, pointing an accusatory finger at Manuel. Her voice was as cold as an iceberg.

Manuel opened his mouth but no sounds came out, his vocal chords paralyzed by Peggy's frosty greeting.

"Oh, baby, this dude and me, we go back a long time," Rick said with a sardonic grin, pulling out a couple of cigarettes from a shirt pocket and handing one to Peggy.

"As a matter of fact, we go as far back as the time when I had that shitty Mickey Mouse paper route, which I passed down to this *spick* like an old, torn baseball glove." He defiantly lit Peggy's cigarette and then his own, blowing smoke in Manuel's direction.

Manuel blushed furiously. "Peggy, I came out here," he said between his teeth, "to let you know who this guy really is. He's not only a bad-mannered moron but a petty thief. I'm doing you a favor by telling you this. He's not worth the ground you walk on."

"Hey, buddy, whatta you think you're doing?" Rick growled, raising a fist and with the other hand grabbing Manuel by the shirt.

Peggy tried to get in between the two combatants, but Rick pushed her away with a swinging arm.

"Hey! Stop it!" she yelled, more at Manuel than at Rick, as if the younger of the two young males was more at fault for the push.

The daily walking and carting of papers around the route, in addition to his weekend basketball playing in pick-up games with friends on outdoor cement basketball courts near his house as well as on the indoor wooden-floor court at a local YMCA, had given Manuel the physical strength, grit, and agility to meet Rick's present challenge adequately and fearlessly.

As Rick shoved him against the side of the school building, holding on to his shirt, Manuel pivoted nimbly on his right foot and, using Rick's momentum in his favor, slammed the older boy's body like a rag doll onto the red brick wall. Rick uttered an "ugh" and then attempted to throw a feeble punch lacking any leverage. Ducking to one side, Manuel easily avoided the anemic blow, his school bag falling to the ground. By then, though, the adrenalin had taken full control of Manuel, turning him into some kind of attacked wild animal.

With great speed and precision, he hooked several punches into the Rick's midsection, like the ones he had seen thrown by Friday-night boxers on TV. The blows landed with such force that Rick doubled over immediately, letting out a horrid guttural sound as if he were about to puke.

Manuel let him stumble away like a crushed insect.

"You're an animal!" Peggy screamed hysterically, her cheeks wet with tears. She threw a protective arm over Rick, who was coughing his guts out, still bent over. "You smacked him where he has an ulcer, you brute!"

"I didn't put the ulcer there," Manuel argued, his body still shaking uncontrollably from the fight. "His heavy drinking did."

A small curious crowd had quickly gathered around the three young people involved in the altercation. By the expression on the spectators' faces, Manuel thought he was being regarded as a heartless monster and the weeping girl and wounded fighter as the innocent victims.

Acutely aware the crowd's potential threat, he picked up his school bag and got ready to scram out of there before somebody called the cops. But before he beat a fast retreat, he was filled with the sudden urge to communicate his last words to Peggy. "He's no good for you, Peggy," he shouted at her. "I've even heard he smokes some strange stuff called pot. I could have made you proud of me, real proud. My name appears in the newspaper real often for all the right reasons. His might soon show up there, too, but as a Most Wanted Person or as an obituary."

Then he started trotting away, hoping Juan's binoculars inside his school bag had suffered no damage when it had hit the ground

So many worthless people along life's path, Manuel thought, inhaling the exquisite fragrance of the camellias as he trekked up the little hill, from whose crest he would finally be able to catch sight of the convent, where his true love resided.

So many thorns and so few flowers—that was what life was all about.

Peggy Thomas had been one of those thorns. Sister Helen, he had come to realize, was the real flower. Hence the bouquet of camellias he was bringing her in a symbolic gesture.

She would clearly understand the message and tacitly forgive his infidelity.

He would not tell her, of course, where he had gotten the idea for his gesture, some movie called *Camille* mentioned often by Mrs. Di Giovanni, who kept urging him to see it if he ever got the chance to do so. Even the opera called *La Traviata*, she had pointed out, had been made out of the story line, which originally had appeared in a novel penned by the son of Alexandre Dumas. In the film version there was a lady called the "Lady of the Camellias", Mrs. Di Giovanni had informed. This woman loved camellias. That was why her gallant lover often brought her such flowers.

Blind to the source of his inspiration, Sister Helen would surely be more appreciative of his florid gift, considering it an original thought.

He would hand her the flowers in the privacy of the convent vestibule and, at the precise moment when she would lean to kiss him on the cheek, he would surprise her and aim for her lips, sinking his mouth into hers. He hoped there would be no other nuns around during the momentous occasion. She would find his kiss irresistible and melt into his arms, allowing him to declare his passionate love for her. She would measure him with her voluptuous eyes and see how he had grown several inches taller and how beard stubbles now gloriously adorned his face and how his voice had developed into that of a manly tenor, like Mario Lanza.

Then, for his masterstroke, he would produce from his shirt pocket the invitation card to the Central Catholic 1966 graduation ceremonies, at which he would be given the freshman Medal of Excellence, the very same invitation card he had previously meant to send his father, who over the phone had excused himself by saying very important business commitments made it impossible for him to leave Miami to come to Lawrence. This last detail, insignificant and distracting, would naturally be left out of his romantic overture.

Sister Helen would reply that she was deeply flattered by the invitation and would accompany him to the ceremonies but that, with respect to his love aspirations toward her, she would need more time to consider. After all, she was a nun.

"Remember Romeo and Juliet," Manuel would reply, trying to give her inner strength. "Remember Anthony and Cleopatra, Orpheus and Eurydice, Tristan and Isolde, Paris and Helen, Abelard and Heloise. They all put love above anything else," he would recite from memory, having spent days preparing the little speech before a mirror. He would finish it off by saying: "Abelard became a monk and Heloise a nun, and they kept on loving each other. If I have to become a monk or if I have to wait an eternity for you, I will," he would say in his best dramatic voice. "I just hope, though, that together we can make this summer the most wonderful one we've ever had."

Manuel pressed his finger into the electric door bell, noticing his hand was trembling. He then shoved one hand into his pants' pocket and looked over his shoulder to make sure that the camellias, held in the other hand, were fully concealed behind his back. He proceeded to clear his throat and grin several times in rapid succession to relax his facial muscles.

Sister Imelda opened the door, her face as expressive as living stone.

"Good morning, Sister," Manuel said in a feeble voice. "I'm very glad to see you again."

She stood sphinx-like under the door frame for the longest time. "May I help you?" she said at last, piercing him with questioning eyes.

"I came to see Sister Helen." The hand gripping the flowers had already begun to perspire. "Is she in?"

"I'm afraid not," Sister Imelda responded, her voice as icy as a blast of cold air from Antarctica. "As a matter of fact, she's no longer with us. She left Thursday when the school year ended."

Christ, he had missed her by only two days! He thought of the flowers. What would he do with them? Whom could he give them to?

"When's she coming back?"

"She's not," Sister Imelda said curtly, the shadow of a smile, like the wing of a bat, flitting over a corner of her mouth.

Manuel swallowed hard, his throat having turned

completely dry. "Has she been transferred to another school?"

"No. She simply left the order," Sister Imelda announced. Then, baring the tips of her teeth in a sort of triumphant grin, she said, "She just never had what it takes to lead a religious life. I knew that the minute I saw her," she added, blowing out a noisy stream of air through her nostrils in holy disgust.

Manuel felt the skies drop down on him like those from the blackest night. But then suddenly something dawned on him: Sister Helen's decision to abandon the religious way of life was an act of liberation for her. She was now free at last to love him in the way he wanted her to.

"I'm glad," he then said, his initial sadness quickly turning into euphoria.

The muscles around Sister Imelda's neck tensed up. "That was a cynical remark. Good day, Mr. Cruz. And please don't come back. Your days at Holy Rosary Grammar School ended a year ago. There's nothing left for you here."

Manuel shot the nun a searing look. "I guess you're right, Sister. With Helen gone," he pointed out, leaving out the religious title "Sister", "indeed there's nothing left for me here."

A corner of Sister Imelda's mouth quivered with intense anger.

"Oh, and by the way, Sister, I wanted to tell you something else," he suddenly said with a grin, bringing his arm around and revealing the bouquet of white camellias. At that point he didn't care what she thought about his having brought those flowers. "I won the freshman Medal of Excellence at the school you believed I couldn't get into, much less survive in."

Filled with raging fury, her eyes glared at him like those on a Medusa. "Well," she said contemptuously, "I guess Central Catholic is a lot easier than I thought."

"No, Sister," he quickly retorted. "You guessed wrong. It's just that I'm a lot smarter than you wanted to give me credit for."

Sister Imelda slammed the convent's front door shut.

Chapter XIII

*H*e had made his decision. He would do it. Sister Helen had made her decision and done her thing. She was his inspiration for this act and for anything else he might do in the future. She had irreversibly become his Isolde. Like Tristan, he had drunk a love potion out of nowhere and become infatuated with his former teacher.

Before stepping into the bathroom to take a warm bath, he had left a vinyl record playing on the LP turntable in the living room. It was *Tristan und Isolde*, another gift from Madama Farfalla. He had set the volume high enough so that he would be able to hear the Wagnerian operatic sounds while he enjoyed a sensuous warm bath in the tub.

He began to disrobe. The stage was set, the lights were on, and the opera was ready to begin. He could not walk away. He could not refuse to take on the assignment of assuming the role of a baritone on this stage.

No one else was home. Esteban had gone out to play, and Maria, Juan, and Pablo were all working overtime in their respective factories that Saturday. The moment was all his. Helen was all his for the taking, like the silver cup of love overflowing with frothy, white fumes imprinted on the LP record front cover of *Tristan und Isolde*. The rising melodious violins sent chills up his spine, at the same time that they drowned out the existence of the exterior world. He, Tristan, would finally imbibe the exquisite, magical potion of Isolde's being. The juice of life would be spilled. *Carpe diem*! Seize the day!

While Sister Helen had been his inspiration for the act, Mr. Devlin had provided the intellectual food to strengthen his courage for this dangerous leap that could catapult him so close to the sun that his wings might melt and his soul, engulfed in flames, might be hurled down to eternal damnation in the second circle of hell.

Mr. Devlin had made it clear, however, that hell in the Dantean form did not exist and that, if it did, it resided inside every human being, along with heaven. According to the Buddhist way of thought, Mr. Devlin explained, dualities did not exist except in their oneness. Good and evil, light and darkness, and heaven and hell did not exist except as the two sides of the same coin. Every evil act had a good side; every good act had an evil one. Reality was dialectical and ended in synthesis. The clapping of one hand was possible and perhaps even unavoidable.

The dichotomy between good and evil was an invention of a people living in the Near East many millennia ago, a people who, for purposes of group survival and cohesiveness, created a distinction as dramatic as possible between themselves and the surrounding known world. Original good intentions, thus, eventually turned into a sickness that metamorphosed itself from Judaism into Christianity and spread like the Black Plague through the Western World to shackle and enslave men's souls.

So when these nomadic people called Hebrews began

to write *Genesis*, their tribe became the Chosen People or good people and their God the One True God, the good god, and everything else became Not Chosen, false, and evil. The religions of the neighboring enemy tribes heavily promoted nature worship, so nature itself became evil. The serpent was a divinity in Egyptian religion; consequently, the Hebrews made the serpent the evil tempter in the Garden of Eden, not only administering a hard slap on the face of Egyptian polytheism but also spitting in the countenance of Nature, since the serpent, in the process of shedding its old skin, best represented, from among all the known animals, the death-rebirth cycle of Nature. Woman, of course, also went through a similar death-rebirth cycle of her own each month, and so she became an accomplice of the serpent in the temptation of innocent Adam by means of the apple, which easily conjured up the image of the vulva, a symbol of feminine love and beauty and Nature and every spontaneous impulse in life. Only procreation remained a good natural impulse, primarily because it added warriors to the fighting ranks of the Hebrew tribe.

Since Nature was evil and God was good, Nature had to be against God and God against Nature. God, therefore, could not be attributed any nature-like qualities. Thus, He could not be female. Thus, He had to be male. With this well-structured system of thinking and seeing the world, the Hebrews could hope to stay together as a tribe and survive the many brutally harsh challenges of the times.

As Manuel's passions continued to rise in unison with his rebellious, lyrical thoughts and the exhilarating musical sounds pouring into the bathroom, he smiled to himself, pleased to see life so starkly naked now.

Thank God for Devlin. There was no sin. Only life. Only experience. Only love. Only death. He would experience life today in its most exquisite form, at its greatest intensity, and, in the process, die, like a snake casting off its skin, only to be reborn.

At last he began what in a fully conscious way he had never attempted before in his life: the act of masturbation.

In his mind's nostrils, Manuel smelled the bouquet of the white camellias, which, scarcely a half hour ago, he had given to Madama Farfalla, who had gasped at the sight of them, obviously thinking he had bought them expressly for her. Their aroma now transported his imagination to the dead fountain on the little bank by the Lawrence River he knew so well.

That was where he would have wanted to set up his tryst with Sister Helen if he had found her in the convent.

When they met again, if they ever met again, they would just look into each other's eyes for the longest time by that fountain. They would grasp each other's hands and start a slow dance, going round and round, each pulling outwardly like moons around an invisible planet, spinning and carving off one overlapping circle after another over the grass near the fountain.

Suddenly, you let go of me and start running off, giggling like a young girl, throwing your head back and glancing at me with coquettish eyes beneath your nun's cap. I also break into a run, and you begin to race around the fountain, which suddenly, as if by magic, comes to life. Several jets of water spring up from it, and your laughter splashes onto my face like raindrops. Your nun's cap flies off, releasing a gush of silky black hair that reaches to the small of your back. You giggle some more and continued sprinting around the fountain, whose streams of water have miraculously turned into white camellias that defy earth's gravity and stay floating in midair while pursuing us.

When I glance back again, I no longer see flowers but the most gorgeous butterflies with white, blue, and red flapping wings. They fly right by me and throw themselves at your black nun's habit, which they eat away with the greatest avidness from top to bottom as you continue to dash around the fountain, which goes on gushing forth more and more camellias that instantly transmute into butterflies.

Then at last you are fully and gloriously naked, and the beauty of your back sucks the breath and soul out of me, and I, a new Tristan tragically in love with his Isolde, am willing to go on like this forever, chasing your exquisite perfection as the embodiment of my sweet eternal punishment in whatever circle I am confined to in the future.

But at the moment this is not hell, but Eden, and you stop at last, fatigued, and I stumble onto you and we both fall on the soft ground pregnant with the fragrance of the fallen camellias that didn't sprout wings.

You rise to your feet, offering me a hand, and then point to a more secluded spot by the stream underneath a tall tree with a cool giant shade. We start our trek in that direction and I watch both you and myself, as if I were a third person. You two walk, as if in slow motion, toward the shady place, your buttocks gently undulating in their most exquisite roundness.

I watch you both from the grass and the earth. I watch you both from the river, for I am the fertile earth and the river of life and death and love. I skim the surface of the stream and slither out of it onto the bank, tempted to tempt you both; for I am the Queen and King Cobra, the closest thing to the Buddha, and I desperately love you.

I creep through the grass and then through the bed of camellias with their divine aroma. Neither of you feels me when I slide up her side and down your back and along the parting of your buttocks. When I bite your testicles and release the venom, you do not scream. Instead you begin to move your hips back and forth and groan with pleasure. My flicking tongue leads the honeyed way, while the thick head squeezes into her, into the love canal, the dark cave, the eternal cathedral, leading to nothingness and bliss, and I am her and I am you and we are one at the center of all and we rock and we dance and we sing in the blessed cosmic explosion of delirious rapture.

Oh, God, oh, God, he was dying! He was so intensely alive he was dying! He was being suctioned into the hole of the eternal moment, aflame with painful ecstasy. He was falling into a fathomless void with his testicles and heart pushed into his brain and all three things throbbing in unison in excruciating joy. And the strange something would not stop, the inexhaustible fountain spurting out a torrent of nectar and flowers.

When, breathless and spent, he opened his eyes again, he gasped at the amount of liquid white petals that lay strewn all over the bathtub and the wall.

In a fit of panic, he immediately set himself to cleaning up the gooey mess with the awful ammonia smell, in case his mother should arrive from work earlier than expected.

Chapter XIV

"I'll bet you anything you'll be the one in next year's shootout duel with Mr. Devlin."

"Why should I be the one?" Manuel said. "You've got just as much a chance as anyone else. Besides, it's hard to predict something that's a year away."

"You're too modest," Mike Bloom said with a soft smile.

"And you're the very best friend a guy could hope for. I have never felt any envy coming from you toward me," Manuel said. "What I get from you instead is warm encouragement, well-intentioned advice, and sincere friendship," he smiled. "Some of the other high academic achievers in our class, however, would probably jump for joy, I'm sure, if they heard I had thrown myself off a bridge and drowned in a river or been run over by a truck."

Mike Bloom laughed. "Oh, don't be so harsh on your classmates. They all love you."

"You said it: 'classmates'. They're not friends. Perhaps there's even a teacher," Manuel continued, "who would join such a celebration if my life ended tragically."

"You're referring to Mr. White?" Mike asked. He shook

his head sympathetically. "Yeah, some of the comments he made during those tryouts for *Hamlet* were totally uncalled for and out of line. They annoyed me just as much as they did you."

"You can't imagine how many hours I spent rehearsing Hamlet's 'To be or not to be' soliloquy," Manuel said with frustration, wiping his mouth with a paper napkin and throwing it down on the cafeteria table. "And all that just to have him say with a sardonic grin, 'Mr. Cruz, I think your style is a bit too intense and effusive for the portrayal of a Danish prince. You're a bit too hot-blooded, I feel, for the part of a Nordic character. A Mediterranean role would be more within your range of possibilities and in line with your personality and background. So perhaps, if I ever decide to do *Othello*, I'll call you for the part of the Moor.'"

"I wouldn't let that get me down, though," Mike said soothingly. "I was a target of his sarcasm as well. 'Ah, Mr. Bloom, I truly and sincerely believe you tried out for the wrong part. Choosing the role of Horatio was definitely a miscalculation. The character of Polonius would have fitted your personality a bit better. I'm sorry to tell you, however, that I already have someone for the part. But don't despair. At some future date I might do *The Merchant of Venice*. I think you'd make a perfect Shylock.' Now can you beat that for racial and religious prejudice?"

"You're right," Manuel said in a tired voice, and, having lost his appetite, put down his sandwich on the wrapping paper lying on top of the cafeteria table. "It'd be so different if Mr. Devlin were in charge of staging the plays. For one thing, they'd turn out more interesting and lively. For another, the selection of the cast would be fair without prejudice against minorities."

"That's never going to happen. Mr. White is chairman of the English department," Mike reminded him. "What's more, he seems to like running the whole show and calling all the shots. He'd never let go of the reins of the theater stage here to anyone, least of all to Mr. Devlin, his nemesis. Mr. White is a control freak."

"Yeah, you're right again," Manuel said, shaking his head. "Life is a funny thing. Mr. White has power but little talent or creativity. Mr. Devlin is talented and creative, plus incredibly charismatic to boot, but has little power."

"That's because Mr. Devlin doesn't want power," Mike explained. "He's a happy-go-lucky guy, a free spirit. He's not power-hungry like Mr. White. Or, as I said, he's not a control freak."

"The hunger for power is born out of an inability to create, I guess," Manuel said philosophically. "On the other hand, creativity kills the need for power. Maybe that's why women are the less power-hungry of the two genders: they have the natural ability to give birth, a most awesome type of creativity."

"That's deep, man," Mike said thoughtfully. "To all this I would add that power-hungry people tend to be terribly jealous of creative individuals."

"So envy rules the day among males," Manuel concluded with a smile, pleased to be engaged in another stimulating brainstorming session during school lunchtime with his buddy Mike. "By the way, who's Mr. White envious of?" he quizzed.

"That's obvious. Mr. Devlin, of course," Mike quickly replied.

"You're very perceptive."

"And that's why Mr. White hates both of us," Mike went on to say. "He knows you and I were Mr. Devlin's favorite students last year, and so he goes after our heads in a symbolic way, as if we were Mr. Devlin's intellectual offspring. That's why we didn't pass the tryouts for the *Hamlet*."

"So John, that fat Pharisee, who hates Mr. Devlin like the very devil, becomes Mr. White's classroom pet and is chosen for the leading role in *Hamlet*. I guess lard and phoniness prevail in Mr. White's kingdom."

Mike laughed. "You know, I wouldn't be surprised," he said suddenly, his eyes lighting up as if he had discovered something important, "if it were really Mr. White who was behind the student petition supposedly started by John to get Mr. Devlin fired at the end of last year. It seemed too well-written for Mr. Porky to have ever put it together all by himself."

"You're not lying, man," Manuel said. "Porky can't write to save his life. What's more, he's such a cowardly conformist he wouldn't have dared attempt such a thing without getting the green light from somebody with authority."

"Somebody like Mr. White maybe?" Mike grinned.

Manuel smiled back. "Do you remember some of the lies spread in that stupid petition that fizzled out in just a matter of days?"

"I still have a copy at home. I stole it from Porky," Mike winked. "Sometimes when I'm bored and have nothing to do at home, I get a kick out of reading it. Let's see. What were some of the more hilarious accusations? Ah, yes, I remember: 'The willful undermining of the most basic moral principles without which our society would collapse into total anarchy.' Something like that."

"Mark-grubbing, semi-literate John could have never written that," Manuel affirmed, "not even if the Holy Spirit had come down upon him to inspire and enlighten him."

Manuel and Mike chuckled together and slapped hands.

"Do you recall any other incredible statements?" Manuel asked.

"Corruption of youth."

"Right. Mr. Devlin, the Irish-American Socrates."

"Blasphemous and erroneous ideas about the origins of our Judeo-Christian religion."

"And what was that thing about Orpheus?"

"Oh, yeah," Mike grinned. "The founder of a secret club called the Orphic Society, which promoted the obsession with death and held night séances at local cemeteries during which the necrophilous poetry of Novalis, Nerval, and Mallarmé was read and attempts were made to communicate with the dead, including a deceased former spouse of Mr. Devlin's."

"Wow! That was quite a statement!" Manuel exclaimed.

"Yeah, a lot of cryptic horse shit!" Mike retorted.

"I bet you not even Mr. White could have written that. It's beyond his range of possibilities."

"So who do you think wrote it?"

"A professional necrophilous ghost-writer hired and paid by Mr. White," Manuel said, keeping a straight face.

The two sophomores stared at each other in silence

for some long seconds and then burst out laughing simultaneously.

"Listen, do you know when Mr. Devlin plays out there on the school basketball courts," Manuel inquired, after the laughter had subsided.

The chat with Mike had improved his spirits a good deal and, if his mood held up, he would want to talk to Mr. Devlin after school about an idea of his he had been contemplating for some time now.

"What's today? Wednesday?"

"I think so."

"Then he'll be out there today." Mike broke into a smile all of a sudden. "Oh, I see. You want to study his playing style, sort of probe him for basketball weaknesses, huh?"

"You're forgetting we're just sophomores," Manuel replied calmly. "Don't jump the gun."

"Everybody says that you and I, the 'Jew boys' as we are now both called without your being Jewish," Mike said, "will be his top students in our junior year and that it's really a tossup between us as to who will finish *número uno* and get to play him in next-year's basketball shootout."

It was a yearly tradition established by Mr. Devlin to play in a grueling one-on-one basketball contest with the junior-year student who had the highest grade-point average in English at the end of the school year. It was said Mr. Devlin was undefeated in this strange competition and wanted to retire from teaching with an undefeated record in that regard, like some sort of basketball Rocky Marciano.

"Deep down inside, though," Mike added, "I know you'll be the one to break the tape at the finish line. You always seem to do that in whatever you set your mind to. If Mr. Devlin thinks it's going to be an easy match with you, he's up to a big surprise. He's used to dealing with effete nerds at those duels. But you'll be a tough nut to crack."

"Come on, Mike. Have some faith in yourself," Manuel said, patting his friend's shoulder. "Remember the opera isn't over until the fat lady sings. In fact, the opera hasn't even begun yet."

Mike Bloom nodded his head appreciatively. "Thanks for being so humble and generous," he replied.

Manuel was the first person to come onto the outdoor school basketball courts, the place where Mr. Devlin annually held his end-of-the-school-year basketball shootout, his symbolic way of glorifying the Roman idea of *"mens sana in corpore sano"*. The fact that no student at Central Catholic had ever beaten him in such a sports duel had apparently spurred some students to complain that the whole concept of it was not fair since Mr. Devlin, while playing as a starting guard at the College of the Holy Cross, had received numerous tips from basketball wizard Bob Cousy, a Crusader alumnus and a Boston Celtic all-time great.

Manuel was about to sit down on an abandoned cement block when he saw Mr. Devlin trot onto the basketball courts, wearing flaming red shorts, a dark red bandanna with white-flower patterns tied around the top of his head, and a long-sleeved blue sweat shirt that read "Save the Forests, Save Mankind".

A stiff, nippy March wind was blowing on the basketball courts, and Manuel zippered up his jacket. He then sat down to watch Mr. Devlin, who seemed quite impervious to the chilly weather. He was reputed to play outside in shorts even in the dead of winter, alleging wearing long woolen gym pants hampered his between-the-legs dribbling style.

Mr. Devlin started his warm-ups, dribbling to the basket for lay-ups, switching hands each time in both the dribbling and shooting process. Then he began firing off some hook shots, again alternating hands. When he finally noticed Manuel, he broke into a big smile and came over to the sophomore, dribbling between his legs.

Manuel rose to his feet.

"Think of the devil!" Mr. Devlin cried. "Are you playing today? It'd be a rare privilege for me if you joined me. I've heard you're a pretty good hoop player. The junior varsity basketball coach told me, in fact, that you could have made the Junior Varsity team if you had wanted to, but you had an afternoon paper route or something."

"I'd love to stay and play," Manuel said, "but I've got to deliver papers, as you just mentioned."

"I understand. So you're here just to observe me, huh? Trying to find a crack in the armor of Agamemnon so that you can exploit it in next year's shootout, Mr. Achilles?"

Manuel smiled shyly. "No, not really. I came to ask you for some advice."

"Concerning what?" Mr. Devlin said, looking at his former student with probing eyes. He let the basketball slip out of his hands and fall between his legs. He slapped it down with his right foot when it hit the ground, freezing it there like a soccer player with adroit feet.

Manuel gulped. "Something I want to write."

"What? An essay? A poem? A short story?"

"Something bigger," Manuel said hoarsely. He cleared his throat.

"And what is that?"

"A novel."

"Ho, ho, ho, a novel!" Mr. Devlin exclaimed, falling with his back against the thick truck of tree whose foliage was undergoing the autumnal phenomenon of multicolor change. "Whadda you know! A high school sophomore wants to write a novel! The next Raymond Radiguet!" He paused and studied Manuel's face thoughtfully. "But then, *why not?*" he said, massaging his stubbly chin with a hand. "After all, I've set for myself crazier things I've gone on to accomplish just as I had dreamed. So why not? Yeah, *why not!*" he cried effervescently, squeezing Manuel's shoulder. "You've gotta go for it, son, if that's what you want! *The sky is your only limit!*"

Manuel smiled happily, remembering those had been Sister Helen's expression as well concerning his future. "How should I begin it, though? I mean, should I make some sort of outline? Or should I just start writing it without any pre-planning?"

"First, you should have a basic idea or plot, okay? For a poem you usually need a basic feeling or mood or image. For the novel the essential element should be an idea or plot, which could be quite rough at the beginning, mind you. In another words, you should have a mini-story or mini-plot in your head. The details you can work on as you progress with your work."

"Fine. I think I have that, but without the ending."

"Don't worry about the ending. The beginning and middle will help the ending wiggle itself free from out of the most secret recesses of your subconscious, like a snake from out of a deep, narrow dark cave. At any rate, may I ask what the kernel of your idea is for your *magnum opus?*"

Manuel swallowed hard. "The relationship between an adolescent and an old Italian lady who's a former opera singer."

"Sounds interesting and promising. Raymond Radiguet wrote about a relationship with a married woman in his first novel *The Devil in the Flesh*. He was eighteen years old when he started it. You're...?"

"Sixteen."

"Wow! Sixteen. I wish I were your age to set a literary record." Mr. Devlin rubbed his stubbly chin and smiled. "You want me to be your Jean Cocteau?"

"Who's he?"

"Oh, never mind. Is this former singer married?"

"No, she's a widow."

"Oh, okay. And is any of the material autobiographical?"

Manuel blushed slightly. "In a way, I guess."

"Nothing wrong with that, you know," Mr. Devlin said enthusiastically. "Goethe called all his works 'fragments of a great confession'."

"Who's Goethe?"

"One of the great immortals standing right next to Dante and Shakespeare in the pantheon of literary giants."

"What did he write?"

"*The Sorrows of Young Werther* and, of course, *Faust*. Read both works if you get the chance."

"I guess I have a lot of books waiting to be read ahead of me."

"You never stop learning until the day you die," Mr.

Devlin philosophized. "Anyway, you mentioned this old lady..."

"Yeah, a former opera singer and a widow..."

"Are you sure she's a *real* former opera singer?" Mr. Devlin asked with a wink, "although it wouldn't really make an iota of a difference if she was or not, you know. In the world of fiction, the reality that matters abides in the writer's mind."

"No, but she *is* a true old *diva* as she calls herself," Manuel said with excitement. "As a matter of fact, I talked to you about her before. She can talk about operas all day long."

"Okay, I remember now. You told me she had sung in *Madame Butterfly*. Is she the one?"

Manuel beamed. "Exactly. She's a resident in my apartment building where I live. She also happens to be one of my newspaper customers."

"That's one of the benefits of being a paperboy: you get to meet a lot of people, a few of whom, now and again, happen to be interesting people worth writing about. Hmm, so you've been studying her as a potential character for a novel. From the light in your eyes," Mr. Devlin prodded, nudging Manuel's ribs with an elbow, "I can tell you there's a lot more to her."

"Well, yes. The thing is her husband," Manuel said, the words coming out of his mouth much faster now, "died a few years back, apparently after shooting himself in the head. Well, I found the suicide gun!"

"You found the gun?" Mr. Devlin said, sounding shocked. "How did that happen?"

"I'll explain," Manuel replied, clearing his throat. "After my older brother married, my mother, you see, wanted to move out of the third-floor apartment we were living in. She kept complaining that living on a third floor was like living in a pigeon house…"

"A pigeon house?" Mr. Devlin chuckled. "That's a good one!"

"… and that carrying grocery bags two flights of stairs at the end of the week after slaving away as a stitcher in a factory for six straight days was back-breaking. Our landlady, in order to keep us as tenants, talked to Madama Farfalla—that's the former soprano whose husband committed suicide—into moving into a vacant second-floor apartment so that we could move into Farfalla's own first floor one, and, apparently, the old lady was more than happy to oblige. Get the picture?"

"Sure. Madama Farfalla had grown so fond of you," Mr. Devlin pointed out, "she was willing to do anything to keep your mother from moving somewhere else and taking you away from her. In operatic parlance, she was willing to make for your sake, and hers, *un sacrificio.*"

"I think so," Manuel said. "In fact, she uses that word *sacrificio* a lot in talking about operas. Anyway, we moved out of the third-floor apartment and into Madama Farfalla's previous first-floor one, of course, only after the landlady had renovated the inside of Farfalla's former place to comply with my mother's request. And guess what I found inside what was to become my bedroom? The very weapon Mr. Farfalla had used to blow his brains out! It was lying on the top shelf of the closet. I can't explain how the workmen who repainted the apartment could have missed it."

"Oh, God, that's awful!" Mr. Devlin cried. "And what did you do with the gun?" he asked with a concerned expression on his face.

"I gave it back to Madama Farfalla."

Mr. Devlin let out a sigh of relief. "Thatta boy! Anyway, out of such terrible experiences comes art. You may be onto something, kiddo! Let your imagination work on the embryo of that occurrence and turn it into a big white whale, a new *Moby Dick* from a teenager!"

Manuel laughed, amused by the exaggerated nature of the comparison.

Around a dozen students, mostly juniors and seniors, had already congregated around one of the baskets. They kept glancing in the direction of Mr. Devlin, as if wanting to know when he'd join them for the start of a pick-up game.

"Listen, Mr. Devlin, you've been very kind with your time," Manuel said. "I won't take up any more of it. I think you're wanted over there now," he informed, pointing with his chin at the students eagerly awaiting the most popular as well as most controversial teacher at Central Catholic High School. "Thanks for the encouragement."

"Let them wait," Mr. Devlin said testily. "Getting back to your novel, I should warn you..."

"Are you sure I'm not interrupting anything?" Manuel insisted.

"Art before sports," Mr. Devlin said epigrammatically. "As I was about to say regarding your novel, I should warn you to be careful not to let it intoxicate you."

"Intoxicate me?" Manuel asked, shifting his weight from one foot to the other.

"Hey, Mr. Devlin, are you playing?" one of the tallest students on the court shouted. "Because, if you are, you're on my team, Mr. D. It's five-on-five, full-court."

"Have somebody fill in for me," Mr. Devlin yelled back. "And don't bother me again, you Philistines. I'm discussing literature." Then turning back to Manuel, he went on to say, "What do I mean by 'intoxicate'? Well, let me answer you in the form of an anecdote."

Mr. Devlin went on to relate a story about a young man who wanted to write a novel. The English teacher alleged that he had heard the story from a close friend. His buddy, whom he didn't name, told him about an incident which almost turned out to have very tragic consequences. It so happened that a certain Wagner, a Korean War veteran and a rather wealthy man by inheritance, had hired a Mexican maid. Her boyfriend, also a Korean War vet and a heroin addict, agreed to do some odd jobs around the house for Wagner, a compassionate and open-minded fellow, for a mutually agreed amount of money. At the end of the week when Wagner set himself to cleaning his vast and expensive gun collection, he found one of his favorite pieces missing, a World War II vintage Luger.

Mr. Devlin puckered his lips and let out a big sigh as if the Luger had been really his.

Something apparently snapped inside of Wagner, and he went berserk over the supposed loss of his precious handgun. It was as if someone had kidnapped a child of his or cut off an important member of his body. So he stuck a sawed-off shotgun into the Mexican maid's chest and forced her to give him her boyfriend's address. Then he got into his pickup truck and burned tires all the way to the guy's apartment.

He knocked on the front door with the end of a baseball bat. When no one answered, he batted the door down, taking swings as powerful as Mickey Mantle's when the Mick had been at the top of his game. He found the vet lying in bed in a junkie's stupor. Most veins on the addict's arms looked damaged from innumerable punctures.

Wagner shook him fiercely, shouting at him, "Where's my fucking gun, you dope fiend? Where's my fucking gun?"

The Korean-vet junkie kept moaning, "I dunno whad da fuck you talking about, man. I dunno whatcha talking about."

"Did you sell it at a pawnshop for drug money, you scum?" Wagner asked, slapping him in the face.

The addict didn't seem to feel a thing. He just kept mumbling, "You crazy moddafucka! Let me be! I dunno nudding you talking about! Let me sleep!"

"Well, maybe this will clear your head, you son of a bitch!" Wagner said, and started smacking him across the head with the Louisville bat.

Manuel's shoulders shrunk and his hands went up as if to evade the bat's impact from the violent tale.

"When blood began to spurt out of the addict's ear," Mr. Devlin said, resuming his narration without seeming to notice the effect his story-telling was having on Manuel, "Wagner stopped the brutal pummeling and beat a fast retreat out of the place, leaving his victim bleeding profusely on the grimy bed sheets."

Manuel saw a heightened rosy color had crept up Mr. Devlin's neck.

Near his house, Wagner saw the Mexican maid waiting for a bus. He stopped his pickup truck and yelled at her that, if she ever opened her trap and squealed on him, he'd do everything in his power to have her, an illegal alien, shipped back to her shitty country.

The addict almost died from the assault, but Wagner was never arrested. Apparently, the addict couldn't remember a thing. As far as he was concerned, he could have been smacked around by an unknown person or hit by a truck. His mind had been in a haze. The maid, of course, kept perfectly mum about what she had learned of the incident.

"And how did you finish the story?" Manuel queried, simultaneously frightened and fascinated by the narrative.

"Who said I was writing the story?" Mr. Devlin complained defensively. He paused for the longest time, as if hooked and paralyzed by some powerful memory. Then suddenly he went on to say, shaking his head: "Well, in any case, the person who was writing the story, whoever that might have been, took the actual incident and made it the climactic point of his work in progress, changing the names of the real people involved and modifying slightly certain minor details for their aesthetic effect but leaving intact the essence of the violent act. But then he decided to add a totally different ending, one in which the protagonist would come home, search the house again, and find the missing gun mislaid in some part of the house he had overlooked, suddenly being struck by the horrifying thought he might have killed someone over a silly oversight on his part."

"Jesus!"

"Tortured by guilt over his having judged rashly and recklessly, he would proceed, with Luger in hand, to go to his bedroom and sit on his bed. There he would allow his mind the simple luxury of a brief review of his life, and when the reminiscing was over, he would lift the barrel of the pistol to his mouth and put an end to his existence."

Manuel cringed. "Christ, what a hair-raising ending! It has the ring of a Hemingway story! Did you—I mean, did the writer—finish the novel and publish it?"

"Who said it was a novel?"

"Well, then, the story. Did he finish the story?"

"Oh, he... he didn't, he couldn't," Mr. Devlin mumbled, his head lowered. Looking at his feet, he stepped on the basketball with his right foot and pushed the ball forward a little bit with the tip of his basketball shoe and then rolled the basketball back, slipping the same shoe very quickly under the ball and flipping it up with a certain flair right into his hands, as soccer players do. He slapped the ball a couple of times with his right hand while holding it with the left. "He started identifying with the main character in such a way, you see, that suicidal thoughts began to obsess him. So he quit working on the story when he was so close to the end he could smell victory."

"Wow! That's unfortunate. If he had turned the story into a novel, it'd would have been a bestseller, I'm sure," Manuel said in awe, "maybe even a masterpiece."

"A bestseller or masterpiece but with a dead author," Mr. Devlin retorted, a strange, lost expression on his face. "You know, the world of the imagination is often plagued by fatal land mines. When you get immersed in it, you should be very careful with each step taken. One small step can lead you to a golden staircase to heaven, or it can lead you to a fast descending elevator with a one-way ticket to hell."

"I'll try to keep that in mind," Manuel said.

Abruptly, as if in a trance, Mr. Devlin started walking away, mechanically spanking the ball still in his hands. Then, just as abruptly, he spun around and, nailing his eyes on Manuel, said in a surprisingly gruff voice: "You *did* return the pistol, *didn't you*?"

"It was a revolver," Manuel corrected.

"Whatever," Mr. Devlin curtly replied. "You did give it back, didn't you?"

"Oh, of course," Manuel answered.

What a silly question! Give it back to whom? The old geezer who had killed himself? I would have had to go to cemetery to do that, for Christ's sake, he thought.

Of course, he had told his mother about it, and she, too, had immediately ordered him to return it to Madama Farfalla, and he had promised he would. But something inside him had told him that Madama Farfalla didn't want it back, that she dreaded it in the same way a person might dread a snake or a ghost, and that, when moving from the first- to the second-floor apartment, she had left it behind on purpose, although he didn't know for what reason. Maybe she had wanted one of the workmen contracted by the landlady to refurbish the apartment to find it and steal it.

And so he had kept it, a shiny, black snub-nosed .38 caliber Smith & Wesson model revolver, secretly hiding it in a corner of the same top shelf of his bedroom closet where he had found it.

"Well, I'm glad you gave the gun back. A firearm is a dangerous thing to have around the house."

"I returned the thing the very next day," Manuel reaffirmed.

"Good," Mr. Devlin said in a flat voice. "And as for your novel, one last word of advice to the wise: Always hold a great deal of respect for the dead and for the very idea of death. Keep in mind that in certain circumstances the underworld can exert a greater pull on the living than earth's gravity. Remember the story of Orpheus, my son. And good luck with your work," he muttered, and started trudging away, his head bent forward as if in deep thought.

Chapter XV

"*L*et's listen to the other opera."

Margarita opened her eyes very wide. "You brought a second one?"

"Sure. We must take every precaution."

She brusquely pushed herself off him on the living room sofa in her parents' second-floor apartment, disentangling herself from his octopus-like embrace. Then, swinging her round face toward him, she said testily: "Are you trying to tell me you want seconds?"

Margarita, his new Cuban girlfriend, a sophomore at Lawrence High School, could be very tender when she wanted to. But sometimes she showed an irritable side, especially when he asked her for one too many sexual favors. She had big round eyes that accentuated her innocent appearance, and that excited him more. He had met Margarita at the Spanish Sunday Mass held in the Holy Rosary Church basement. He had been her first boyfriend and he had liked this idea very much as a guarantee of her physical purity.

"Please don't get upset," Manuel soothed. "It's not nice, even in a moment of sudden anger, to refer to our act as 'seconds'. It lowers it to the gastronomical level when it deserves to be raised to the lofty heights of an opera."

"There you go again with your big words," she feebly complained. "To think that, when I first saw you at the Spanish Mass, you looked so innocent and down-to-earth and sweet. What a box full of surprises you turned out to be!" she grinned.

"Innocent and down-to-earth I am no longer, but my sweetness depends on you. When you sing to me, I turn into pure honey."

"You sure have a smooth tongue, don't you?" she remarked, playfully frowning.

"No, *you do*," he retorted with a suggestive smile.

She shook her head. "Do you really think I enjoy this under the present circumstances," she whined softly. "Why can't one performance a night be enough for you?"

"Because *my blood is cursed*," he said in a horror-movie voice, histrionically opening his eyes wide, "just as my father's blood is cursed. We are both very hot-blooded."

"*I'll* say. I think you were born with a dairy farm down there," she quipped, pointing at his crotch.

"I can't help it if I love you," he cooed.

She creased her lips to show her skepticism. "Do you really?"

"With all my heart. *Con todo mi corazón. Con tutto il mio cuore*," he told her in three languages, with the flourish of a hand that fell on the left side of his chest over his heart at the end.

She smiled appreciatively. "You're indeed a smoothie."

Manuel sighed noisily. "One day we'll have all the

privacy in the world we could want. Then both of us will be able to enjoy ourselves freely. For now, though, we can't take any added risks."

Margarita listened attentively. She always did whenever he began to speak in a soft, paused, low monotone. When he spoke in such a way, the look in her black eyes, no matter what the subject might be, would change. A storm might be raging through them, but his voice would have a calming effect on them and turn them into placid lakes. He knew of his hypnotic-like verbal powers over her and did not hesitate to use them whenever he felt they were called for.

"You've got to understand that I work very hard with my mind," he proceeded to say in a mellow voice, "and so I, more than most people, need moments of personal relaxation and enjoyment, such as the ones you so exquisitely and selfishly offer me."

"God, I love to listen to you," she said gently. "When you talk like that, you sound like a poet or a philosopher."

"Thank you. Take today, for instance. I woke up very early this morning to study and prepare for the upcoming SATs. Then I worked on the body and conclusion of an English paper for Mr. Devlin based on a comparative study of Marlowe's *Doctor Faustus* and Goethe's *Faust, Part I*. All that just about consumed my Saturday morning. Around noon it started snowing. I watched the thick snowflakes fall gently past my bedroom window, and all of a sudden I wanted to rush out and run on the snow like a little kid, watching the footprints I would leave behind, and throw a few snowballs at lampposts. The snow reminded me of Winnetka, Illinois, when I was a ten-year-old living with an American family. But, of course, I couldn't go out. I had to work on my novel. And that's what I did all afternoon long."

"Oh, yes, *your novel*," she said in a critical voice, "the best kept secret in the world. You say you don't like to talk about it because it's bad luck. What's the title of it again? *Cristóbal and...* what else?"

Apparently, she found it so funny that a mere teenage should try to write novel that she covered her mouth with a hand.

"*Cristóbal and the Madama*," he said in a tight voice. "Later on," he continued, disregarding her silly, immature behavior, "I knocked off a letter."

"A letter? Now wait a minute," she said, sitting straight up and fixing him with her large, dark eyes. "Whom did you write the letter to?" she asked, throwing back her shoulder-length straight black hair.

"Ah, well, ah," Manuel stuttered. "To my... ah, father. Since long-distance telephone calls went up, I've been writing to him rather often," he explained, meeting her challenging stare unflinchingly until her eyes backed off.

"That's strange" she said. "You're always telling me how much your father has made your mother suffer and how much you hate him for this and that. You wouldn't be planning to imitate your father and make me suffer, would you? I hope you're not writing love letters to some other girlfriend of yours on the side," she said, her eyes hardening.

"Of course, not," he said, hugging her. He kept silent for a discreet amount of time until Margarita had finally calmed down. Then he popped the question again: "Would you sing for me again now?"

"Okay, but your microphone is probably dirty from

the first performance," she pointed out tiredly, using the secret code words he had created for their lascivious activities in order to confuse anyone in her family who might try to eavesdrop on them from the next room.

"Don't worry. I'll clean it," he said calmly. "I always bring an extra handkerchief. But first let me put on the other opera on your record player."

He rose and walked over to the console, on top of which lay the opera albums. He opened the sliding door of the cabinet of the console, which included not only a phonograph player and radio but also a twenty-six-inch television set. He removed the second record of the first opera, Arrigo Boito's *Mefistofele*, and slid it back into its album cover. Then he took out record one of the second opera, Charles Gounod's *Faust*, dusted it off with a handkerchief, and then lowered it to the platter. After setting the tone arm onto the playing surface, he returned to the sofa, still holding his handkerchief.

"You're not going to use the same hanky you wiped the record with, are you?" Margarita cried, glaring at it with disgust. "I don't want dust in my mouth."

"I said I brought two hankies," he said. "So relax. I always come prepared for any situation."

"What opera is that?" Margarita asked, yawning.

Manuel smiled. "Gounod's *Faust*," he answered, as he wiped his exposed penis with the clean handkerchief.

"Sounds a little bit like the first one—depressing!"

"Somber and melancholy, maybe. But definitely not depressing. It'll get better, though. Just relax. You'll see."

"If you say so," she said, quite uninterestedly.

"Both operas essentially deal with the same trio of main characters: Faust, Mephistopheles, and... and

Gretchen," he said, changing names in midstream as a certain parallelism dawned on him. "Both Boito and Gounod based their operas on Goethe's *Faust*. Gounod used only Part I, while Boito included Part II also. I prefer Gounod's version because it has a tragic ending. Boito's ends on a positive note with Faust being saved. Despite the mushy ending, the wonderful figure of Helen of Troy appears in Boito, and I think that's the work's saving grace."

Margarita broke into girlish giggles, which, instead of getting Manuel upset, sent electric shivers down his spine.

"You know," she said, after her giggling has subsided, "I listened very carefully to what you just said, but somehow the more I listened to you, the more confused I got," she confessed.

"It's important," he replied in a syrupy voice, sliding the handkerchief into a pocket in his pants, "that I explain these complex things to you. With time you'll come to appreciate them," he added, feeling the erection coming on again.

Hidden behind the protective wall of beautiful orchestral and voice sounds, he would be able to enjoy the moment to its utmost, moaning and groaning rapturously, his mind engaged all the while in a flight of fancy taking him to the ends of the world, if need be, to the Greek islands themselves, in search of his beloved: Helen, not Sister Helen anymore, but just Helen, *his* Helen.

"Promise me one thing," she pleaded.

"Anything, anything," he whispered, already feeling the strong surge of passion.

"Next time could you please bring a Mozart symphony

or Chopin piano concerto or any other type of nice instrumental music?"

Margarita knew how to play the piano, and so there was a certain logic to her plea.

"Oh, yes, yes. It's a wonderful idea. But please sing for me now. I'm dying for you to sing for me!"

And she sang and her song was sweet and divinely exquisite, but his imagination, on wings of delirious ecstasy, flew off to another goddess, his divine Helen.

Oh, Helen, why have you abandoned me? I have consecrated my heart and soul to you, and you do not answer a single letter. I am risking my sanity and the salvation of my soul, and you do not even drop a simple line on a postcard. Since the day I lost my virginity, the virginity of the heart and soul, I have stopped going to confession, and so my soul is now banished from the holy sacrament of Communion and from the Holy Roman Catholic Apostolic Church. All this and more I have given up for you, my goddess, yet with silence you answer my desperate love cry.

I know you have not moved. Some months ago I went back to the convent where I first laid eyes on you, deity of my being. I visited with Mother Superior. I asked her to verify your address, which she had furnished me over a year ago. She confirmed that it was the correct one and that, furthermore, as far as she knew, you had not moved. So there you are. My curiosity still unsatisfied, I queried if she had received any letters from you lately, and she said yes.

That, my love, truly crushed me.

When I asked for your phone number in a moment of desperation, I was bluntly denied the request, and right then and there the lights almost went out for me and all my hopes.

But somehow, as your distant faithful lover, I have managed to keep the faith and to persist in writing you letters expressive of my innermost needs, desires, and dreams toward you, letters which, on occasions, I have sprinkled with the aromatic dewdrops of my desperate passion and then sent to you. I would die for a meager scrap of a letter from you. A letter of mine sent back stamped "Return To Sender, New Address Unknown" might even give comfort to my hopes. But nothing. Only absolute silence.

Sometimes I am struck by the suspicion that there's a dark, jealous secret lover intercepting and destroying the amorous labors of my pen. If he exists, please recognize he'll never compare with me or my love for you, which is as infinite as the stars.

I am writing a novel, and you are in it. In fact, you are the Helen of Troy of my work. One day fame will be mine on account of this fictional work, which is more real than fictional, on account of you. Your name then, like the immaculate flower that you are, will bloom on the lips and minds of millions of people everywhere in the world. They will read about my love for you, my precious idol.

Please come back to me before it is too late. Do not leave me abandoned in this hour of deepest loneliness, like some youthful Christ on the cross. Look at me from below. Make those eyes your eyes and that mouth your mouth, as I surrender to you myself and my spirit and the nectar and seed of my eternal love.

"Oh, God! Oh, God!" he cried, holding Margarita's head down until he was empty.

Then he reached for the fresh handkerchief, and

Margarita spit into it, making a horrible face. As she buttoned up her blouse, she looked at him, and her countenance, like a sun coming from behind a dark, rain-pregnant cloud, suddenly burst into a shining smile.

"You're crying," she observed with a concerned look.

"Out of love for you," he said, feeling deeply exhausted and sad.

He heaved the deepest sigh.

Chapter XVI

"How's your masterpiece going, young Goethe?" he asked, launching a shot that swished through the basketball net.

"Fine, I think," Manuel said, throwing back the ball to his teacher. "The other day something really weird happened, and it has really fired up my imagination."

"Well, that's good. Tell me about it," Mr. Devlin grinned, firing off another jump shot from about fifteen feet away and banking it in.

Manuel returned the ball. "A couple of weeks ago I stepped out to get the mail at home. The mailman handed me a Holy Cross catalogue along with some other mail. I was so happy to receive the catalogue I didn't bother to check the other mail until I was back inside the apartment. Then and there I noticed a letter that didn't belong to me or my family. It was addressed to a certain Floria Giordano. Since it was time to go do my route, I grabbed my paper-route bag and rushed out, hoping to catch the mailman if he was still in the neighborhood. But he was nowhere to be seen. I waited around a bit out there on the sidewalk in case he popped out of some other apartment building, but no luck."

Mr. Devlin nailed in another shot, this time from about twenty feet away. "Go on," he said. "I'm listening."

Manuel snapped back to him a crisp two-handed pass. "Still I decided to walk up a block or two and see if I could still track him down, but the results were the same. The man had absolutely vanished. I didn't want to lose any more precious time, so I continued on my way to the *Eagle-Tribune*, where I picked up my bundle of newspapers. From there I went on to do my route."

Manuel told Mr. Devlin that it had been Friday, meaning payday. Mrs. Di Giovanni, a customer of Manuel's not known for being a tipper in any sense of the word, had needed to break a dollar. As Manuel had pulled out some coins out of a shirt pocket, the letter had fallen out and dropped on her bed. All it had taken had been a second or two for Mrs. Di Giovanni's hawk-like eyes to zero in on the letter and spot the name.

"*That's her!*" she shrieked, clamping her claws down on the envelope. "That's her!"

"What is it?" Manuel said, totally confused.

"That's her!" she repeated, now grinning from ear to ear while examining the writing on the envelope very carefully.

"Is she a friend of yours or something?" he asked.

"A *friend*?" she said, and then broke into a deep throaty laughter that sounded almost masculine. "Sure. Sure. A friend! An excellent friend, in fact!" Then she grabbed Manuel by the shirt and asked: "Tell me, where did you find this?"

"In my mailbox," he answered in utter befuddlement.

"What I suspected. And, tell me, where do you live?" she said, releasing him.

Her sharp eyes remained fixed on his lips as if to force him to tell the truth and nothing but.

Manuel told her, and her face lit up again, like a detective's would do on TV when he has suddenly realized who the murderer was. She then went on to explain that she had always known where Floria Giordano lived and all of that but that she had lost all communication with her right after some tragic event occurred. Afterwards, Floria's phone had been disconnected. Now, however, a golden opportunity had arisen with the knowledge that she again had a go-between, a messenger, to keep both women in touch with each other.

"Well," Manuel said, "in that case I'm sure you'd like for me to keep the letter and return it. It should help renew the friendship."

She laughed again. "Come on, you silly boy. Haven't you understood yet?" she said. "This Giordano woman is your soap opera lady, your so-called Madama whatever."

"It's Madama Farfalla," Manuel corrected, not liking the mocking tone Mrs. Di Giovanni had assumed, "and she's a former opera singer and a wonderful lady."

"Oh, is that what she is? A lady?" she smirked at him, while she proceeded to push several coins into the palm of his hand.

It was the exact payment, not a penny less, not a penny more, for the delivery of a week's worth of newspapers. She closed his fingers and pushed his hand away, as if she had given him pure gold.

"One day," she promised, "I'll let you know who this Madama Farfalla of yours really is. *A lady*, ha!"

"When?" Manuel immediately asked. "When will you tell me?" The words appeared to have tumbled out of his mouth.

"When you're good and ready," she answered.

Manuel went home pondering all of this. Meanwhile, his curiosity about the letter kept growing and growing until he could hardly resist the temptation of opening the envelope and seeing what was inside. So when he got home, he took a kitchen knife, went directly to his bedroom, and slashed the envelope open. What he read in the letter found inside was indescribable!

Mr. Devlin looked at the Manuel for the longest time after the narration was finished. Then, all of a sudden, the English teacher broke for the basket, dribbling with his right hand and attaining maximum acceleration when he was precisely underneath the basket. At that point he leaped up with tremendous spring, gyrating in midair beneath the rim and laying the basketball softly with his left hand against the left side of the backboard for the layup, his fingers lightly tapping the rim as a finishing flourish.

"You don't seem to suffer, I see, from white man's disease," Manuel joked.

Mr. Devlin paid little regard to the comment, picking up his own rebound. "So she was writing letters to herself, huh?"

"Gosh, how did you guess?"

"And she wrote them as if you, Manuel Cruz, were writing them—a son writing homesick letters to his mom."

Manuel's jaw dropped. "You're more incredible than I thought! You're more incredible than... than Madama Farfalla! Now wait a minute! Did somebody tell you all this?"

Mr. Devlin smiled mysteriously. "Keep in mind I'm your Master."

"But that's mind-reading, for crying out loud! That's practically *ESP!*"

"Maybe," Mr. Devlin replied softly, and let go of another shot that ripped through the net like a missile. "But in reality everything in life has a scientific basis," he added. "Remember the time you told me you were made to write frequent letters to your mom when you were living with an American family in Winnetka, Illinois? It was Winnetka, wasn't it?"

Manuel nodded, astounded, and stared at his English teacher in awe.

"Well, you could have told Farfalla the same thing, and from that she got her idea for what she did."

"Incredible! The fact is I did tell her."

"Get the ball!" Mr. Devlin suddenly ordered with a sudden sternness. "You get the rebounds until I miss. Playground rules."

The teacher's command, sharp as a slap on the face, shook the student up.

"Sorry," Manuel said. He retrieved the ball and hurled it back to the teacher.

"You know, while you were talking, I kept hearing this music," Mr. Devlin said.

"What? An opera?"

Mr. Devlin grinned. "No. no. A symphonic poem by Paul Dukas. Walt Disney used it, as a matter of fact, in *Fantasia*. The piece is called *L'Apprenti sorcier*, which translates into..."

"I know," Manuel interrupted. *"The Sorcerer's Apprentice."*

"Good."

"The name sounds a bell," Manuel said, "but I really don't know what it's about."

"The little musical drama is based on a ballad by Goethe. It talks of the relationship between an apprentice and his master, who happens to be a magician. The apprentice invokes a spell to obtain water, but the forces he lets loose get out of control and result in a terrible flood, which only the master magician can stop. Get the message?" the teacher asked, taking his eyes off his target for a second to glance at Manuel, enough time so that the trajectory of the shot was upset, the ball caroming off the rim and missing the basket.

"Not really," Manuel chuckled, "but it's my ball now and my turn to shoot."

Mr. Devlin shook his head, trudging toward the basket to assume rebounding duties.

His legs well rested and full of coil, Manuel leaped high into the air and delivered a jump shot that felt perfect and looked perfect in its arc and backward rotation. It burst through the net so explosively, it made the net spring up and get caught on the rim.

Mr. Devlin took a few steps back to get a little running room and then dashed toward the basket, jumping at the end of his run and pulling down the net.

"Not bad, kiddo," Mr. Devlin smiled, picking up the ball and passing it back. "You can leap and shoot, and you can even write good essays. Who knows? You might even turn into a great novelist."

"Thanks."

"By the way, speaking of Holy Cross, I heard you want to follow in my footsteps and go there."

"Hopefully," Manuel said humbly, swishing in another jumper.

"You know why I went there?" Mr. Devlin said, scratching his stubbly cheek.

Maybe Mr. Devlin had forgotten to shave that Saturday morning, Manuel thought. But most likely the former Crusader simply had had no time for shaving, being that the "shootout", upon his request, had been set up for nine o'clock that morning, and, furthermore, the place agreed upon as the site of the game, a quiet, isolated park in Andover, also a Devlin idea, was a distant drive from Lawrence. In previous years the Devlin "shootout" had always taken place on the outdoor cement basketball courts at Central Catholic High School.

Maria had driven Manuel to the park, complaining all the way that the whole arrangement had to be the concoction of a lunatic mind and that she would never again do Manuel such a favor for his own good. When she had asked what time she should come back to pick him up, he had responded that he'd ask Mr. Devlin to take him home.

"No. Why did you go to Holy Cross?" Manuel said.

"Because of the name," Devlin explained. "I thought, and still think, everyone should go through some sort of crucifixion sometime in his life as a learning experience, as something to put hairs on his chest. As good old Nietzsche once said, what doesn't kill me makes me stronger."

"Did they crucify you on the hill?" Manuel said kiddingly. He knew the college rested on a hill, overlooking Worcester.

Mr. Devlin looked at Manuel with a rather serious face. "No. That came later."

"Where? In Korea?" Manuel asked, and immediately regretted having asked the question.

He had heard that, as a twenty-three-year-old infantryman there, Mr. Devlin had been captured and later tortured by the communists. But the word out was that Mr. Devlin always stiff-armed anyone's attempt to bring up the topic of his war past. Once he had even denied, it was said, that he had ever been to Korea. At any rate the Asian war, as well as the recent death of his third wife, was a subject off limits to everyone.

Mr. Devlin's face had turned to granite.

"Sorry," Manuel said in a thread of a voice. He then swished another shot and later had one hit the rim and bounce up but still fall through the basket.

Mr. Devlin cleared his throat and forced a stiff smile. "So we have another Crusader in the making, huh," he finally said after, it seemed, the longest silence. "I have the most wonderful memories of the Cross. In fact, it was there I had my most significant religious experience."

Manuel held back his shot, glancing at Mr. Devlin to see if the teacher's somber mood had changed. After all, hadn't Devlin once said in class that religion was the most subtly efficient way of keeping people from having a religious experience? And hadn't he even nodded his head with keen delight when Manuel had remarked that in Machiavelli's *The Prince* it was stated that religion was the most effective way of keeping up appearances? Yet now Mr. Devlin was talking about a "religious experience" he had had at the Cross?

"It was in a basketball game in my senior year," Devlin went on to say in a perfectly serious tone of voice. "That morning when I woke up, something told me I'd have an incredible game that night against Fordham, that I would be unbeatable. And the truth is I practically shot the lights out of the place."

From the very first shot he took that ripped through, all net, Devlin knew some radar inside his head, never before used by him, had been switched on, some third eye of his, never before opened by him, had been awakened. He stopped seeing the ball itself. He saw only rings and circles, rings going through rings, circles going through circles, time going through the hole of eternity. It was weird, uncanny.

He had never dunked before in his life, but that day on a steal and a breakaway, he went up for a layup and just kept going up and up and up. He seemed to be levitating himself off the floor, off the face of the earth, and then he knew he was living the greatest moment of his life in that Holy Cross-Fordham game. So he let go of himself and pumped the ball behind his head with both hands once and slam-dunked the baby home, grabbing and hanging on to the rim like a gorilla, like Tarzan. The Crusader crowd went absolutely wild.

By the end of the first half Devlin had scored forty points, shooting a torrid seventy-seven percent from the floor and not missing a single foul shot. Then in the locker room, he told his coach that he wasn't coming out for the second half. The coach almost flipped.

"You have to be nuts," the coach said. "You're poised to break the school's all-time individual scoring record and set an unbeatable new one, scoring eighty, ninety, maybe even a hundred points in a single game, like Wilt Chamberlain did when he was a Philadelphia Warrior. Tonight for you," he said, "the sky's the limit."

The sky was the limit, the coach repeated. He'd issue strict orders so that Devlin would be the only Crusader shooting in the second half. Devlin would be fed the ball constantly, while his teammates would set up all kinds of picks for him all over the floor, single picks, double picks, triple picks, whatever he needed to set the new unbreakable record. "You'll make history tonight, by golly!" the coach cried, making a fist.

By that he meant, of course, that he, the coach, and Devlin, the player, would make history together. The coach wasn't being as selfless as he sounded.

"Thanks," Devlin said, "but, no, thanks."

He had known the perfect moment, without single, double, or triple picks, and that was more than enough— for him at least. Furthermore, he didn't want to ruin it with a less than perfect performance in the second half. So he started dressing up.

The coach yelled he'd suspend Devlin for five straight games or the rest of the basketball tournament or maybe even kick the college student off the team for good. Devlin shrugged his shoulders and started walking toward the showers.

In a huff, the coach left the locker room to return to the playing court with the other players. His threats against Devlin, however, were never carried out.

"I played in the next game and had an off-day," Mr. Devlin now said. "I was out of rhythm for some reason and scored a meager total of thirteen points for the entire game. Never again during the rest of my college basketball career did I have a basketball night like the one in which I scored forty points just in the firsts half. I never came even close to it."

With Manuel having missed a shot, the ball went over to Mr. Devlin, who now paused in his speech to swish in a beautifully arching jumper.

He smiled at Manuel before speaking again. "And you know what? Today when I woke up, I strangely felt the same way as on that day when Holy Cross beat Fordham and I was practically unstoppable."

Manuel chuckled. "All that gabbing just to try to psych me out, huh?"

"We'll just have to wait and see, won't we?" he said with a small smile. "You ready?"

"Ready as I'll ever be," Manuel replied, screwing up his courage.

"Up to twenty-one? Gotta win by two?"

"Okay. Everything goes back except a steal, right?"

"Fine with me."

"Dear teacher, you're on."

"You look kind of confident."

"I am," Manuel said a bit hoarsely.

"Then let's play for some stakes."

"What'll they be? A couple of beers?" Manuel said good-naturedly. "I haven't reached the legal drinking age yet."

Mr. Devlin nodded his head. "I'm perfectly aware of that."

"Then you set the stakes," Manuel said with growing bravado. "What have you got in mind?"

"Let's raise the stakes to proportions in which the game will become exciting and suspenseful. Maybe even *deadly.*"

Manuel gulped. "What?"

"Let's go for all the marbles," Mr. Devlin said.

"Whadda you mean?" Manuel said, tilting his head.

"Let's bet our lives on the outcome of the game."

"You can't be serious!" Manuel complained in a trembling voice.

"If you win, you kill me. If I win, I kill you," Mr. Devlin said, the most ungodly expression on his face.

"You've *gotta* be pulling my leg," Manuel laughed nervously, scrutinizing the teacher's face. "*Please say you are.* I don't want to start thinking you've suddenly gone wacko," he said, remembering his teacher's supposed Korean War past.

"I mean every word I say: Let's play for our lives."

"I'm going home," Manuel replied.

"You can't. You don't have a car and it's me you've asked to take you home."

"I'll walk if I have to."

"Too far to walk. You'll reach Lawrence after the Fourth of July, and you'll miss the celebration with all the fireworks there. We're in Andover, remember."

Chapter XVII

o that was why Mr. Devlin had chosen a distant park in Andover! Manuel thought with anguish. "I'll hitch a ride."

"And then tomorrow I'll read in the newspaper: 'Teenage hitchhiker was found strangled to death in a ditch.'"

"The Boston Strangler is behind bars."

"Maybe not. Maybe an innocent man is behind bars."

"I'll call the police and tell them everything."

"They'll think you're insane."

"This is really getting ridiculous," Manuel said disgustedly. He suddenly turned his back to the man and started walking away. He didn't care if he reached Lawrence by Christmas. All he wanted was to get away from this nut.

"Why are you leaving?" Devlin yelled at him. "Are you leaving because you find the 'shootout' ridiculous or because you're scared stiff? And you want to be a writer, huh? You'll never make it. How can you? You're just another Francis Macomber. You're afraid of the lion! You'll never finish that crappy little novel you're working on. You haven't got what it takes. You're the Mickey Mouse of your own 'Fantasia'! You're the apprentice in Paul Dukas' work. You're gonna have to call back the master, the magician, me, who's paid his dues many times over, to help you finish what you can't complete. You'll need me desperately to come up with an appropriate conclusion to your endless sophomoric novel!"

Manuel stopped dead in his tracks and put his hands on his hips. He turned around very slowly and then began walking back very fast, something already in the process of smoldering inside him.

Mr. Devlin was undoubtedly a frustrated writer who had never managed to finish a real book. On the other hand, Manuel was well into the process of writing one that would catapult him precociously onto great heights of fame and glory one day when it was published. He would show the basketball has-been as well as the writer manqué who was who on the basketball court now and at a later date on the literary scenario.

"Alright, you're on," he said in a sharp voice. "I take it out first."

"No special privileges for anyone," Devlin replied stiffly. "No princes here, no sacred cows. We shoot from the free-throw line to determine first takeout rights."

Manuel's hands were trembling so much, he missed his shot from the foul line.

Devlin banked his in and took the ball.

"Oh, incidentally," he said, "I have several very efficient killing instruments in my car trunk. If you win, you may have the choice of the following: an M-1, a .38-caliber revolver, perhaps like the one you found in your new apartment, a Luger, a machete, a samurai sword, and a dagger," he enumerated with the greatest aplomb, as if he were merely naming the dogs or cats he kept as pets at home.

Then he commenced his dribble, sliding from side to side with his back to Manuel.

Manuel guarded him cautiously, keeping himself bent low, his center of gravity pushed forward, a hand lightly touching the man's back to be alerted by both touch and sight if Mr. Devlin made a sudden move.

Manuel was not taking any chances. He would play the hardest game of his life, no matter what. For, even in the case his teacher was putting up a terrific acting job in trying to play a wild ruse on him, even if the whole verbal setup constituted the biggest prank ever played on a high school junior, even if his life were in no way threatened, other things were definitely still on the line, namely, his reputation, his ego, his pride, and his honor. Now more than ever, since winning the Medal of Excellency for the third year in a row, he had a name and a stature to maintain. Surely, he would hate to hear bruited around the school hallways in his senior year that he was an effete bookworm with no heart and guts who had lost to an old man on a basketball court.

"You know, somehow I still don't get the feeling," Mr. Devlin said, pounding the ground with his hard dribble, his back still turned toward Manuel, "that you're truly convinced this is a real war, that we are battling for our very own lives. But so that you may have a more graphic idea of what you're up against, please be informed I have picked the .38-caliber revolver as my weapon of preference for administering my *coup de grâce* to the future loser, meaning you."

Having said this, Devlin, in a flash, pivoted to his left, faking a drive down that side. Having easily caught

Manuel overcommitted in that direction, he reversed his dribble, simultaneously spinning his body with the ball, and went to his right for the unopposed layup and the easy score.

"One, zip," he said with an icy grin. Then he added in a derisive voice, "I already smell a corpse."

Manuel tapped the ball back to him, frightened but hardly disheartened. Twenty-one points was a long way to go. A thirty-nine-year-old man would surely run out of gas half way there. Manuel would bide his time, not getting desperate, and deliver the knockout blow in the later rounds when Devlin would be holding on to the ropes, gasping for breath and mercy. Then having won the match, he would ask the man very politely for the samurai sword to give it an operatic finish.

Facing Manuel and leaning forward while sharply bending the knees, Devlin began a very slow dribble from hand to hand. Slowly, he increased the tempo of the dribble until practically the ball became a blur. Manuel maintained a degree of distance as protective measure against the fake. Then Devlin suddenly feinted with his head to the right, and Manuel moved half a step back. A full body fake to the left drove Manuel back another half step. On the third feint, the very moment Manuel pulled back once more, Devlin gyrated freely and leaped straight up, catching the student flat-footed.

The soft jumper swished in.

"Two, zip."

Manuel's heart began to beat faster. He bounced-passed the ball to Devlin, who stared at him with menacing eyes.

"Kiss the valedictory speech for next year good-by," Devlin said darkly.

Taking a deep breath, Manuel wiped the perspiration breaking on his forehead. He then positioned himself in a much tighter defensive stance against Devlin, who all of a sudden started dribbling away from Manuel and the basket until he had reached a distance of about twenty-two feet away from it. Suspecting the teacher had something up the sleeve, Manuel remained stationed where he stood, tacitly challenging the other to shoot from so far away—which Devlin proceeded to do, launching a missile with amazing accuracy and rotation that zipped cleanly through the hoop.

"Three, nothing," Devlin announced with a blank face.

A series of well-mixed Devlin lay-ups, hooks, and jump shots, aided by deceptive head and body moves and fancy dribbling, raised the score to an ominously disproportionate level.

"Seven, zip," Devlin said in a toneless voice. Then forming the letter "T" with his raised hands, he requested a timeout, adding, "Don't go away. I'll be back shortly after the commercial."

In a growing state of confusion, distress, and paralysis, Manuel watched him walk toward his car. If psyching out his student, or his "apprentice" as he had derogatorily called his top academic junior student in English literature, was his objective, Manuel mused, he was efficiently succeeding at it so far. Not even in his worst nightmare scenarios had Manuel imagined such a lopsided beginning to the shootout. Frankly, he had to admit he was getting plenty scared. Furthermore, the recall of the nasty rumors that had circulated around the school concerning the private life of the unconventional

English teacher was not helping his concentration or his courage any way.

"Devlin is death-obsessed," he had heard a Central Catholic student affirm.

"Korea did a number on his head," another student had stated.

"He killed a bunch of chinks over there. Life means nothing to him now. He's seen too much shit got down. Hey, man, I'd rather mess with an alligator than with that cat any day of the week."

"It's no secret he worked for the CIA. That means he knows how to kill you and make it look like you died from a heart attack or something. I wouldn't be surprised if he actually killed his third wife. She died from a heart attack, you know."

"He's into some weird California satanic cult he joined while a grad student at Berkeley," John, alias Porky, had asserted with great satisfaction, adding another element to the long list of allegations about the idiosyncratic teacher.

When he saw Devlin strut back from the car, holding a black revolver and a small white box, Manuel felt his guts tremble. An inner voice told him to run for it, but another counseled that an attempt to flee would make things much worse. Suddenly, he remembered the time on his Winnetka paper route when he had been bitten by a dog, precisely because he had tried to pedal too hard to get away from the menacing canine. Flight here, however, might mean getting bitten by a far more dangerous breed of animal, a human animal, a snake with hypnotic blue eyes and deadly venomous fangs. This animal now had a gun in his possession.

Manuel tried to move a foot and open his mouth, but

no part of his body seemed to respond. It was as if he had been fully stripped of his will.

Devlin laid the gun and white box on the grass a foot or so from the edge of the basketball court and about four feet from the basketball pole. He then sauntered back to the playing field.

"Just in case you pull a 'Francis Macomber' on me and turn tail," he said, staring at Manuel with cynical eyes. "The ball, please."

This was really getting serious, Manuel told himself, *deadly fucking serious.* So he now fought against his physical and emotional paralysis head on, taking little jumps from side to side as tennis players do about to receive a hard serve, slapping his chest as if he had football pads on, growling and grunting like a mountain gorilla. He had to get his blood pumping, the oxygen flowing, the adrenalin raging, his heart and soul screaming.

This was not just the battle *of* his life. It was a battle *for his life.*

Devlin started a slow deliberate dribble, his back as usual turned to Manuel, who threw an arm around the right side of Devlin's body as a decoy move and then made a lunge on the left, stripping the ball away.

Since it was a steal, Manuel did not have to take the ball back across the foul line. Being within his shooting range, he decided against penetrating and shot an outside turn-around jumper.

The shot lacked the high arc. In fact, it was more like a line drive, but he had leaped so high, he had felt he was shooting downward instead of upward. The ball exploded through the net.

"One, seven," he cried, pumping a fist into the air.

The real Manuel was back, he told himself.

"Alright, apprentice, just don't get too cocky," Devlin grumbled, returning the ball.

Manuel developed a quick short-range battle plan. He would not penetrate yet. It was too extenuating and dangerous. On penetration one worked harder, got banged up more, and became more vulnerable to blocks and steals.

He would increase his score a bit, shooting from the outside. He then proceeded to hit two jumpers in a row from fifteen feet away. Three, seven. Devlin, however, extended his defensive perimeter, forcing Manuel to shoot from farther away. In spite of this, Manuel scored two more shots from twenty feet.

"Five, seven," he said with glee.

"You don't know what you're getting yourself into," Devlin warned, wiping his sweaty palm on his red shorts. "Just don't get me mad."

He threw the ball back at Manuel, expressing deep disgust either with himself or toward his opponent.

Now Manuel decided to penetrate, but as he drove past Devlin, he felt something from behind him gently flick at the ball, which went out of the control of his hand, hitting his foot and rolling out of bounds.

"Damn it!"

"Out on you," Devlin called. "You've gotta lot to learn, kiddo."

Manuel knew no limits had been set on fouls. That meant he could foul Devlin as many times as he wanted to without fouling out and forfeiting the game. The only thing that could happen was that Devlin might get mad and punch him or something. But what was a punch compared to getting shot in the head?

So he now stuck to Devlin like wallpaper, flapping

his arms around the man's sides, lunging at the ball, pushing a leg into the opponent's backside, slowing down the enemy's movement by grabbing the opponent's t-shirt with an artful hand. Devlin kept slapping away at Manuel's persistently pressing, clutching tentacles.

One slap glanced off Manuel's forearm and hit him in the face.

"Ugh!" Manuel cried, his hand instinctively flying to his face. When he brought his hand down, he saw blood on it.

"Shit, man, I'm bleeding. You scratched my face!"

"Go home and run to mommy, you poor little boy," Devlin said in a mocking voice as he went up for a free layup. "Eight, five."

Now Manuel was mad, ripping mad; the treacherous devil had grossly taken advantage of a delicate situation.

And so Manuel's defense grew rougher, almost violent. He began to use his hands and knees with more ferocity. He discovered his elbows as an equalizing weapon and on one occasion landed a solid blow with his right one on Devlin's mouth. The brutal impact threw Devlin on his butt.

He rose quickly, shaking the cobwebs out of his head and checking his mouth for any fallen or loose teeth. The damage inflicted there was merely a cut lip, and no foul was called.

Blood, added to profuse sweat, had begun to flow on both sides.

When the score reached fourteen to thirteen in Devlin's favor, the teacher called another timeout. Manuel thought his opponent would go for a drink of water, and he, quite frankly, was ready to follow suit, but the man did nothing of the kind.

Instead, he walked over to the gun, opened the white box, and began to insert bullets into the revolver's cylinder.

Manuel fought against a sudden fainting spell. Devlin laid the gun back on the grass and returned, bleeding from the cracked lip and scratches on his chest, neck, and face. His white jersey was tainted with blood, probably a mixture of both his and Manuel's, and showed a tear on the side, a product of the youth's holding tactics. He looked more bloodied and bruised than the student and actually seemed to represent the part of a boxer who had gone through some grueling rounds with an unscrupulously clawing, scratching, elbowing mauler of an opponent with the mentality of no holds barred.

The battle was quickly resumed, with every new point leaving each combatant wearier and more banged up by the minute but at the same time more fiercely and desperately determined to eke out a victory at all costs.

Manuel tied his enemy for the first time at eighteen but, in order to conserve whatever ounce of energy he had left, he made no gesture of celebration and defiance.

Then Devlin stole the ball from him and threw a left-handed hook shot that seemingly came out of nowhere and took a shooter's bounce on top of the rim and managed to tumble in. The slap of the basketball hitting the hard pavement after going through the hoop sounded like a hammer's blow driving yet another nail into Manuel's coffin and heart.

Devlin asked for the third timeout, panting and gasping for oxygen. Manuel himself felt so fatigued and out of breath, he was willing to concede a five- or even a ten-minute break before he might collapse dead on the ground. But again Devlin did the unexpected, once more walking over to where the gun lay, picking it up, and bringing it over this time onto the playing field, where he gingerly deposited it on the cement court in the middle of the center circle some forty-odd feet from the basket.

"The circle," Mr. Devlin muttered, mostly to himself, "a symbol of infinity and eternity, the serpent biting its tail."

The man was insane, *absolutely insane*, Manuel thought, and he, Manuel, was only two points away from his death at the hands of a homicidal maniac gone mad on account of his war experiences. He surrendered the ball to his potential future murderer and immediately attacked, stealing the ball and, in the process, fouling him grossly.

Devlin remained eerily silent and calm, his face an expressionless mask of death.

No foul being called, Manuel kept the ball and, in a sudden deceptive move, drove for the basket. Devlin partially blocked Manuel's running jumper, but the shot had so much rotation on it, it still succeeded in squeaking through.

"We're even-steven," Manuel said very hoarsely, feeling dehydrated.

Devlin lunged at the ball and stole it, but Manuel called a foul and got the ball back without any verbal protest from Devlin, who merely shook his head.

Devlin lunged again, this time stealing the ball so cleanly that, when Manuel realized he had been stripped of his prized possession, Devlin was already dribbling away toward the basket for another score.

"Twenty, nineteen. *Game point!*" the executioner

announced with vicious alacrity, the words sounding more like *"death point"*.

Manuel suddenly felt he was asphyxiating. He was taking deep breaths but something seemed to be blocking the oxygen's path to his lungs. The court had turned into a gas chamber where Manuel, the Cuban Holocaust Jew, was about to be gassed with mustard and cyanide. He looked around for help, but the remote park with the basketball court was as deserted as a lost island in the Pacific Ocean. No cars, no pedestrians. Too early in the morning that Sunday for anyone to have roused himself out of bed in the few scattered houses in the area. Devlin, the Devil, had picked the right place and the right time. Only one option might remain for Manuel under the looming possibility of his loss: to shout at the top of his lungs with the distant hope that someone might hear him and come to his rescue.

But he couldn't, shouldn't, think of defeat at that moment. The fat lady had yet to sing.

Devlin took the ball and dribbled slowly toward the gun lying on the playing field at the very center of the basketball court.

Manuel froze where he stood, frightened and confused.

Devlin positioned himself behind the gun and, remaining stationary, continued dribbling, dribbling, dribbling. Then the cruelest smile broke on his face, and he stopped the dribble, taking the ball into both hands.

Then Manuel gasped, realizing the man's next diabolical move.

And Manuel sprinted for his life, lowering his head like a bull, aiming his horns for the *torero*'s gut, running and yelling like a savage. As he made his frantic rush with his head bent forward and low, he rolled up his eyes to watch his human target, who slowly, methodically, deliberately, raised the basketball and, from behind the head, flung it forward, using the right arm like a powerful sling.

But Manuel kept rushing forward, thinking only of goring and destroying the threat to his life. The very moment he slammed his head into the other's gut, he spun to get a last glance at the demon's rainbow that augured death.

The ball of time went through the hole of eternity.

All net.

Immediately Manuel clutched the man on the ground with one arm and with the other starting throwing wicked punches at the defenseless ribs.

"*You mothafucka! You mothafucka!*" he cried.

Then the image of the gun flashed through his brain. He immediately rolled to his left, and when the back of his body struck it, he jumped to one knee, grasping the firearm with both hands.

With one leap, he was straddling his executioner.

Tears splashing onto his cheeks, he poked the gun into the hateful face, shouting, "I'm gonna kill you, mothafucka! I'm gonna kill you! *You deserve to die!*"

With the barrel pressed tightly against his cheek, Devlin could hardly talk. Still he managed to say, half-gagging: "Don't... shoot... there... Shoot... here."

He pointed at his chest with his only free hand.

Manuel lifted the barrel slightly off his opponent's face.

"I want funeral services with an open casket," he pleaded with greater ease.

Manuel's hands were shaking uncontrollably, at the

same time that he kept blinking to drive the tears out of his eyes.

Devlin kept perfectly still.

Suddenly, another gush of tears fully blinded Manuel, and, terrified, he pulled the trigger.

The horrible explosion threw him back, as if he had been whacked across the chest by the heaviest hand. Above the ringing in his ears, he heard the soft trickle of laughter. Again he blinked and saw, beneath a slender snake of smoke curling out of the mouth of the gun's barrel, what appeared to be tiny pools of tears in Devlin's eyes.

Or were they mere reflections of his own tears?

Manuel dropped the gun onto the ground and slowly stumbled away toward the wire fence.

Hanging on to the fence, he wept openly and freely.

When he stopped weeping, he felt an arm around his shoulders.

It was his teacher.

"Come, my son," Mr. Devlin said in the gentlest voice. "It's time to go." Then after a long pause, he added: "If you've survived this, you'll survive anything."

Suddenly, Manuel gyrated, throwing off the teacher's arm, and punched his victorious opponent in the stomach one more time.

Chapter XVIII

*M*aybe he should have thrown it into the river a long time ago. But, on the other hand, he would not be even thinking this if he had returned it to the wife of its former owner as soon as he had found it. Now he could do neither. Slowly and quietly growing and gathering strength in the concealing darkness of the closet, it had attained a voice and personality of its own. The shiny, black metallic serpent now seemed to be calling all the shots with respect to its own existence and even that of its new illegal owner. It seemed to have a power of its own to hypnotize the soul and neutralize the will. So strong had its witchcraft become that Manuel could not even bring himself to dispose of the four remaining bullets, true bullets, real McCoy's, not blank cartridges like the ones Mr. Devlin had used to scare the hell out of him the day of the "shootout" at an outdoor basketball court in Andover.

Manuel tightened his grip on the thick metal threads of the wire fence, gazing over the small bank with the dead fountain toward the gently flowing stream.

To be perfectly frank, he could not even pinpoint the

exact moment in his life when living for him had become such a high-wire act. But undeniably it had become just that, with potential dangerous repercussions, not only for himself, but also for people close to him. Lately, as a matter of fact, he had begun to feel like a walking time bomb, like a terrorist without a motive or a cause.

It was definitely a good thing his father had departed from Lawrence before his mother, with tears welling in her eyes, had dropped the horrible news on him: The night before his departure, Manolo had finally confessed to her that he had fathered a child with his mistress. Maria had been harassing him for the truth for quite some time, and that was what she had eventually gotten from him—nothing but the truth—to her dismay. It had come out *just like that*, as if he had been telling his wife the most natural thing in the world, like the weather forecast for the Southern Florida area during the next several days!

Swoosh! A large dagger rammed into Maria's heart and Manuel's! How insensitive on his father's part! Manuel thought.

No doubt, the witnessing of his mother's pain and frustration had deeply shaken Manuel. Nonetheless, he felt something else had disturbed him more: the haunting thought that another being, another creature, even if it were only a mere crawling baby, had come into the world with the potential to monopolize his father's love.

Fuck the bastard child! *Fuck his father*!

For days jealousy had raged inside Manuel's soul, putting all kinds of homicidal ideas in his head as he reminisced about the night when he had been awakened by the squeaking sounds coming from the box-spring bed in his mother's room. Sneaking out of his bed, which he had temporarily shared with his smaller brother during his dad's brief stay, and pressing an ear against the common wall, he had heard his father bellow, "Take the sweet *leche de tu toro, mi vaca!*" How crude! How animalistic! If he had had *una estocada* at that moment, he would have rammed it right between the eyes of the clamoring bull.

After his father had left Lawrence, Manuel's anger had slowly turned into a red-hot hatred riding on wounded male pride. By then he had wanted to jump on a plane and fly down to Miami to hunt down his father, willing, like a kamikaze or a samurai warrior, to slay the dog wherever he found him, at home, in the office, or at some crossroads.

Manuel heard thunder and, releasing the fence, started walking back to the apartment. As he began his return trek home, he glanced up and saw the twilight summer sky quickly darkening with menacing clouds. Feeling a sudden swift breeze laden with the smell of rain, he accelerated his gait.

Manolo had left looking happy and satisfied, Manuel remembered. He apologized a thousand times at Boston's Logan Airport for not having been able to come to see his son receive the Medal of Excellency award for the junior year at the June graduation ceremonies at Central Catholic, but he promised he would return for sure the following year for his son's graduation, where, he was sure, his progeny would deliver a stunning valedictory speech.

Let him come next June, Manuel bitterly mused, taking another quick glimpse at the blackening sky. Just let him. He should consider himself lucky that he made it out of Lawrence alive and on his own two feet and not dead and inside a casket. For his luck Manolo should undoubtedly thank Maria. She had astutely delayed telling her son of her husband's new paternity until Manolo was safely a thousand miles away.

As he was about to enter his apartment, he heard someone call out his name. He looked to his left and upward and saw Madama Farfalla standing on the staircase landing.

"You do not come this afternoon," Madama Farfalla smiled without covering her mouth. "You forget it is Friday?"

"When I left the paper, I knocked but apparently you weren't home," he explained.

"I go to the music store. You have supper already?"

"Oh, yes."

"How about an after-dinner coffee then? Yes?"

"Alright," he said tonelessly, and started climbing the stairs. "It looks bad outside."

"Why bad?" she asked, trudging up beside him while holding up her long black skirts. "Is rain bad?"

"I guess it'd depend on your point of view," he admitted, "wouldn't it?"

"You've grown much," she smiled. "Here and here," she said, touching his head and heart. "But more here," she added, tapping his head again.

"Alejo Carpentier, a Cuban writer, alludes to the varying perceptions of rain in one of his works," Manuel pointed out. "Urban man sees rain as a nuisance, Carpentier says. On the other hand, the farmer, more attuned to nature, sees rain as a blessing."

"And you also are a blessing," Madama Farfalla said, "*to me.*" She touched his cheek and then opened the door to her second-floor apartment, which, within a very short time after her moving into it, had been transformed into an almost exact replica of the first-floor one before the latter had been surrendered to the Cruzes: a tomb-like cave of musty darkness.

The first thing that caught Manuel's attention as he entered the dimly lit kitchen was a colorful album resting on the kitchen table. It was Puccini's *Turandot*. When he returned his gaze to Madama Farfalla, he saw she was smiling broadly without covering her mouth. She had stopped shielding her mouth sometime back, allowing him to see freely the tooth gaps that pockmarked her smile.

"Take it," she said softly. "It is yours."

Manuel sighed and shook his head sadly. How could he get mad at her for playing little silly games, using his name to write letters to herself, when she was so nice and generous and perfectly harmless?

"How could I ever repay you," he said, "for the wonderful musical education you've given me?"

"You repay me? For what? For opera records nobody listens to anymore? *Assurdo!*" she said. "You do not owe me. I owe you. That reminds me. I have to pay you for the newspaper, *non è vero*? It is Friday. I go get *il denaro* now and then make the coffee."

Manuel sat down at the table and looked at the album cover. In the half light and with difficulty, he studied the soft pastel colors that served as background for the artwork on the album cover, as well as the figure of the Chinese woman, placed in a lower central position there, who stared directly and defiantly out in a frontal direction with icy slanting eyes and tightly sealed lips and who somehow reminded him now of his coldly silent

Helen, the Helen of his dreams, the Helen of his never-answered letters.

The Oriental woman was wearing a brownish headdress from which, on either side, protruded the neck and head of a small dragon. Behind her on a mural was painted a much larger twisting brownish-yellowish serpent.

Madama Farfalla returned and paid Manuel, leaving him a hefty tip. So accustomed had he become to her generosity, he merely said in a voice empty of excitement, "*Grazie.*"

"I hear you singing last night," she said, pattering over to the gas stove to begin the coffee-preparation process. "Your room is right below mine, of course. The song was the Cavaradossi aria *E lucevan le stelle.*"

"Yes, that's right," Manuel said embarrassedly. "I hope I didn't give you nightmares."

"No, *solo l'opposto.* I dream with angels. You sing that aria very beautifully. Your voice improves every day, you know. It would improve even more if you would take lessons with Madama Farfalla," she smiled. Then her expression turned serious. "Last night, however, you sing in a... yes... very beautiful but also very different way. Last night your voice sounds very sad, very sad. It never sounds as sad before."

"It's a sad aria. If you recall, Mario Cavaradossi sings it in a prison cell as he waits for his jailers to come get him at daybreak for his execution."

"I know, I know. I was Floria in *Tosca,*" she said, placing the filled coffee pot on one of the burners on the stove, which she proceeded to switch on. "That was *molto tempo fa.*" Then turning around and fixing him with her big black eyes, she added in a concerned voice, "What

I mean is this: Last night you sing like you are about to be killed, like you are about to go before *un plotone d'esecuzione.*"

A firing squad. Had he sounded that depressed?

"I have a very strong imagination," he explained, averting her eyes.

"But I still worry. *L'immaginazione* is a dangerous thing."

"Did you hear that?" Manuel suddenly said in a not too subtle attempt to divert the focus of the conversation.

"What?" She had returned her attention to the coffee.

"The thunder. Did you hear it?"

"Oh, that. I do not hear it. I feel it. Ever since this morning I know it is going to rain today."

"You probably read the weather forecast in yesterday's paper," he said skeptically.

"I do not need a paper for that," she replied in a very serious voice. "I live on a farm in Italy when I was a little girl. I know *Madre Natura.* Maybe I go out later when it rains," she said as an afterthought.

"You'll get soaked, I'm telling you," Manuel warned. "From the looks of it outside, it's really going to pour."

"So what?" she said defiantly.

"So what? So you'll catch pneumonia!"

"And?"

"Don't you have a singing engagement in the coming days?"

"At La Scala, you mean?"

"Uh-huh," he grinned. "Weren't you going to sing the part of Cio-Cio San?"

She squeezed his hand playfully. "I cancel. The money is bad."

"Ah, okay. Well, then, you'll catch pneumonia and die!"

"*E che cosa è la morte?*"

"Ah, let's see. Death is a state of non-being."

"Oh, I see. So you come back up from down there, eh, Orfeo, and you say you see nothing down there, huh?"

Manuel laughed softly. The old lady did not look highly intelligent, but in truth she was a smart cookie, a sharp whip, with an extraordinary memory.

Then, all of a sudden, he realized, to his satisfaction, that he had probably laughed for the first time since his mother had revealed to him his father's terrible dark secret. Something inside of him, it seemed, was now again reawakening, coming back to life, so to speak, at the same time that he was gradually beginning to feel communicative and, yes, almost happy once more.

"By the way, my main character is committing suicide at the end of the novel," Manuel confessed, finding the revelation appropriate since the topic of death had been broached.

"You cannot allow that," she immediately replied in an unusually stern voice, slapping the table a few mere inches from his coffee cup.

The severity of her words, the stiffness of her voice, and her explosive gesture all combined to startle him.

"Why not?" he mumbled. "Aren't operas full of suicides? Doesn't Cio-Cio San kill herself at the end of *Madame Butterfly?*"

"We must go out tonight," she said, as though not hearing his questions. "It is a need, a big need—*for you, for me.*"

"Out where?"

"To the river. To the fountain."

"In the rain?"

"Yes, yes. *Precisamente*. We need the rain."

He felt tempted to say, "That's crazy!" Or, more strongly still, "You're nuts!" But he checked himself and instead simply complained, "My mother would kill me."

"A silly exaggeration," she retorted. "No mother kills her son. But a son can kill a mother. A mother dies for her son. A mother is all sacrifice, *tutto sacrificio*. A mother is love." She smiled suddenly, shocking him again with the dark gaps in her withered mouth. "Besides, I have a parasol you may use."

Abruptly, she rose to her feet. "*Piove*. There is no time to lose," she implored, a note of urgency in her voice.

"Strange. I don't hear it," Manuel muttered.

He tried pricking up his ears but still heard nothing. Then, all of a sudden, a stiff, whistling wind banged into the apartment building and shook its windows, followed by rain pelting against the window panes of Farfalla's apartment.

Perhaps the heavy curtains and the window shades, he thought, had muffled the first sounds of the striking precipitation, or perhaps somehow the half-deaf old lady had truly heard it or, rather, had *felt* it, *smelled* it, *intuited* it, *imagined* it, before it had happened.

Strange old lady indeed.

It was an Oriental parasol what Madama Farfalla brought out.

"Japanese," she specified with pride. "A memento from my opera days as Cio-Cio San."

"That thing looks very fragile," Manuel chuckled. "It'll fall apart in no time."

"Maybe not. Anyway, it does not matter. The rain is good for you," she insisted. "*È un balsamo per l'anima.*"

A balm for the soul. The old woman could turn quite lyrical under the weirdest circumstances.

"The rain will clear your head," she went on to say. "You have too many ideas in your young head. The rain will clear your head of dark thoughts. It will lighten it. I do not want it to crash or explode."

Manuel gulped. "I'm sorry, but, for heaven's sake, could you please tell me what we're going to do out there?"

"*Pregare.*"

"Pray? In the rain? Does that make any sense?"

"We will sing and we will dance. Song and dance—they are forms of prayer."

Manuel shook his head. "That's crazy."

Madama Farfalla handed him the Japanese parasol. "I am ready. *Andiamo*," she ordered firmly.

"Aren't you putting on a raincoat or something?" he asked, growing more disconcerted by the minute.

"No need," she answered stiffly, taking him by the arm. "*Andiamo.*"

"Wait a minute. I'm not sure about this thing yet. Let me think."

"You think too much. *Andiamo*," she repeated, tugging at his arm.

Outside the rain was coming down hard, bouncing off the pavement like liquid pellets. Manuel opened the parasol, offering it to Madama Farfalla, who pushed it away. Then they started walking toward the river.

The driving rain bombarded Manuel's shoes and pants, soaking them in seconds. Madama Farfalla, since she was holding on to Manuel's arm, was partially protected by the parasol, but it was obvious she did not seek its protection. In fact, she appeared quite intent on getting thoroughly soaked from head to toe as quickly as possible.

When they reached the street corner, she paused a minute to pull her head back and to one side, open her mouth wide, and gulp down a mouthful of rain.

"Do you remember that song in the first act of *La Traviata*," she asked as they crossed the street.

"You mean the drinking song?"

"Yes," she said. "*Esattamente.*

She had given him the Giuseppe Verdi opera in LP album form after he had mentioned he had watched the movie *Camille* with Greta Garbo and Robert Taylor on television. She had informed him both the movie and the opera *La Traviata* were based on Dumas' play *La dame aux camélias*, which he had later read, he remembered, in the original French with the aid of a French-English dictionary. He also recalled that, when she had asked him what had motivated him to see the film, he had said his curiosity had been aroused when he had seen it announced in the newspaper, although the real reason had been that Mrs. Di Giovanni had pricked his interest by insisting so many times that he see the classic and study very carefully the character of the "Lady of the Camellias".

No need to create needless jealousies and rivalries, he felt.

"The song that begins: '*Libiamo, libiamo ne' lieti calici...*' That one?" he asked.

"*Si. Precisamente.* You remember that song?" she said with excitement. "It is wonderful, very wonderful song! A most happy song! A drinking song about youth and *il amore* and *il vino*. A most appropriate song to sing tonight. You know it well?"

"Yes," he laughed. "It's one of my favorites and I have a good memory for songs."

For the first time that evening, he was beginning to like the little crazy adventure. For one thing, as she had foretold, it was clearing his head. He was laughing. He was forgetting his "problem".

"You are youth," Madama Farfalla said, touching his upper arm.

"And you are, of course, *il amore*," Manuel chuckled, with an exaggerated gesture of a hand.

"And the wine?" she said, arching her glistening eyebrows. "Where is the wine?"

"Oh, I know!" Manuel exclaimed. "The wine is the rain!"

He laughed again, feeling happy once more and beginning to love the wet little game they were playing like children. Never in his life had he done something as crazy as this.

"Rain is very sweet," she commented. "It is the sweetest thing in the world. Why do you not taste it now?" she prodded.

"Alright," he smiled, and stuck his head out of the parasol, opening his mouth wide. He pulled his head back to face the night sky and swallowed. "Gee, you know, this reminds me of the time when I was a kid in Cuba and my school took our class on a field trip to the countryside. There we bathed and swam in a river. The water was very cold and also very sweet and delicious. I had never drunk water as sweet as that *until now!*"

She pressed herself hard against him. "Do you not think we know ourselves before?"

"In what sense do you mean?" he said, glancing quizzically at her wet face.

Under the rain her countenance seemed to be going through a transformation. With her black hair dripping wet, her face radiant with rain beads, her huge eyes catching the filtered light of the full moon and sparkling like stars, she appeared to be turning strangely young.

"In another life?" she whispered. "Do you believe in reincarnation?"

"Hmm, reincarnation? Gee, I don't really know. I haven't thought about it much."

"It is not what you think. It is what you *feel*. Do you feel we know each other before in another life," she asked again, rephrasing her question.

He looked at her and was overwhelmed by an odd, indescribable sensation inside. "Yeah. Maybe. Why not?"

"I feel I am your mom perhaps in another life," she speculated wistfully, lightly tapping his shoulder with a finger. "Maybe that. Maybe something else. Maybe once before we are a couple of tigers running together through an endless *giungla*." She roared like a tiger, making Manuel laugh. "But for sure we know each other in another life," she asserted categorically.

Manuel remembered the secret letters she wrote to herself under his name, and he couldn't make a reply. A knot had formed in his throat.

When they reached the schoolyard by the river bank, Manuel spotted the three homeless dogs that often hung around the school area and slept in a place protected from the elements by a concrete roof that jutted out over a rollup door through which food deliveries for the school cafeteria were received. Neighborhood kids called the canine drifters the "Three Musketeers".

The "Three Musketeers", apparently jittery over the

heavy rains and the occasional lightning and thundering, started barking, in unison, at the unexpected visitors.

"Sing to them, Manuel," Madama Farfalla asked. "Sing to them and you calm them."

Manuel began to belt out Alfredo's part of the duet in the *Libiamo* drinking song, and, sure enough, the barking ceased and the three canine heads, as if belonging to one body, vanished in the darkness.

"*Bravo!*" Madama Farfalla cried, releasing his arm and clapping. "*Ancora! Ancora!*"

He took an operatic bow, holding on to the parasol.

Manuel went through the hole in the wire fence first, almost ripping the parasol on one of the loose thick wires. Then he helped Madama Farfalla squeeze through, offering a gallant hand. While she bent forward to pass through, he could not help catching sight of her pendulous heavy breasts. A top button on her dress, apparently, had either burst loose or been left unfastened. She was wearing, he also noticed, no brassiere.

"Sing '*Libiamo*' again and dance with me," she pleaded, extending her arms.

"What will it be? A waltz?" he smiled.

"*Si. Un valzer.*"

And he sang and they danced while she laughed and giggled like a happy young girl. They danced in circles, and when they came to the dead fountain, now full of rain water, they danced around the old structure. He held on to her tightly for fear she might trip on a hole or rock, fall, and break an old fragile bone, while she raised an end of her long skirt with her left hand and thrust back her head to catch rain on her radiant face and in her open mouth.

He sang the Alfredo part of the duet many times

over until he stopped and said, "What happened to the chorus? What happened to Violetta?"

In a weak and slightly hoarse but very sweet and melodious voice, she accompanied him on the chorus lines.

But then suddenly, when it was time for Violetta to sing her aria, he felt Madama Farfalla's ribs powerfully expand with the heavy intake of air, and from the old woman's throat broke forth the most beautiful live operatic sounds he had ever heard from such close range.

He gasped and stared at her in disbelief as they continued to go around in circles and ellipses. How could her singing voice, so long dormant, not have suffered the ravages of time? Did she train her voice in secret inside her lugubrious apartment, camouflaged underneath the high volume of her record player? Or did she practice some strange witchcraft to keep her throat in such Dorian Grey form?

They kept dancing and singing, and when Manuel stumbled on a word or line, she would whisper or sing it for him.

So wrapped up in her incredible voice did he become that a sudden gust of wind managed to rip the parasol from his hand and send it rolling down the bank and into the river before he had time to make a dash for it and recover it.

"Oh, do not worry," she soothed, sensing his embarrassment. "That is nothing. *You* are everything," she said, stroking his soaked hair while she gazed into his eyes with great intensity.

They continued dancing. Then suddenly she started doing the leading and gently began guiding him toward the trees.

Then, when they were only a few yards from them, she stopped singing and dancing and he followed suit, and she led him by the hand toward the tallest tree. When they reached it, she leaned with her back against it and, without releasing his hand, whispered: "*Questa notte divina è la più bella e felice di vita mia.*" She then raised her huge eyes at the full moon partly concealed by a black rain cloud and, letting go of his hand, lifted her arms until her hands, making perfect arcs in the upswing, met above her head. She brought the arms down slowly, and when they were shoulder-high, she extended them forward and beckoned him.

As if hypnotized, he drew closer, and she pressed his head against her wet breasts.

"I can *feel* a nest up there on one of the branches," she said, and pressed his head harder against the warmth of her bosom, which abruptly began to heave as if a volcano were erupting underneath. Then a hand slithered under his face and pulled at something, and Manuel felt naked flesh against his mouth and cheek.

The sky lit up and thundered, and he lifted his head and, under another discharge of lightning, saw how she continued to tear away at the top of her dress, until she was completely naked from the waist up. Huge flashbulbs up in the sky kept exploding with delayed thunder, and suddenly her hands, lightning-fast, clutched his head and pressed his face toward the large sagging breasts with the broad dark nipples, as she cried, "Drink my milk! *Bevi, bevi, mio figlio!*"

He did not struggle until he felt her hand force a nipple into his mouth.

"*Mio figlio, bevi, bevi!*" she screamed with rapturous

joy, as a sour milky substance was squirted onto his tongue.

"*Bevi il mio latte, la mia anima, la mia vita!*"

When he at last managed to free himself after a long struggle, Manuel ran on the swiftest pair of feet that had ever carried him, wiping his mouth and glancing back not even once.

Chapter XIX

It was he. There was no mistake about it.

And so immediately all kinds of questions invaded Manuel's mind: how he, a professed ardent anti-communist and former CIA agent, had snuck into the socialist island; how he had managed to find his former student's house in Caibarien, Las Villas, Cuba; why Maria, who considered the man nuts, had allowed him inside the house; why he had come on such a strange visit; why he had retired from teaching at Central Catholic High School; and what he might had been doing all these months wherever he had disappeared to.

"Hey, long time no see," Manuel cried, feeling, for God knew what reason, a little nervous and awkward in front of his former English teacher, who had played on him the cruelest hoax anyone could imagine on that desolate basketball court in Andover, Massachusetts. "What have you been up to? I heard you had gone off to Europe to do research on Ludwig II of Bavaria and write a historical novel on him. Is that really true?"

"Well, yes. But... but how did you find out about it?" Mr. Devlin mumbled.

"Oh, I've got my connections, you know," Manuel

replied with an enigmatic smile. "My father worked for a while with the CIA in Cuba, you know. So the 'Mad King', huh? An opera fanatic. Of course, you wouldn't consider this sudden peculiar interest of yours a mere coincidence, would you?"

"In what sense?" Devlin said suspiciously.

"Well, in the sense that it's kind of odd that the central character in your novel should be an opera fanatic and the main character in mine is a former opera singer named Madama Farfalla," Manuel said in a sarcastic voice. "You're not trying to imitate me, are you? Ran out of ideas for fictional characters or what?"

"Oh, speak of the devil Madama Farfalla. Has she gotten here yet?" Mr. Devlin said.

"She's come to Cuba, too?" Manuel said, deeply puzzled.

Devlin nodded his head, his lips pressed together very tightly. "We've come to finish what we couldn't back in the States," he explained, as he pulled out a snub revolver from a pants pocket and brandished it in front of Manuel's face. "We're sure that on this lawless island we can get away with murder."

Manuel reacted immediately, making a dash for his very life, bullets whizzing past his ears. To make himself a harder target to hit, he ran in zigzag fashion, while keeping his body bent forward as low as possible.

When he reached the last room of the house, the kitchen, he rushed out onto the patio and then onto the backyard, where Madama Farfalla stood waiting for him, holding a huge handgun with the largest barrel he had ever seen, something obtained perhaps from an African safari hunter. She held the lethal weapon by the side of her long black skirts, while smiling her toothless smile.

Manuel sprinted for the mango tree and climbed it like a monkey, using hands and feet. When he reached the top branch, he looked downward.

Both Devlin and the old lady by then stood beneath the tree, their grinning evil faces turned upward toward Manuel. Devlin's little pistol was gone, but around his body was curled a huge, fat cobra with flicking split tongue and all. With the most barbarous peal of laughter, he released the serpent, which began to writhe up the trunk of the mango tree, while the old lady raised the safari revolver with the gigantic barrel and aimed at a single spot: the cross point where the line of his eyebrows met that of his nose.

Manuel gasped so hard, his heart shrunk into a tiny knot of fear, and the rest of his body followed suit.

Suddenly he was no longer a human being but a tiny worm crawling swiftly under great fright toward the tip of the branch to escape from the snake twisting up the tree and the other stiff and more deadly metal serpent, Farfalla's gun. Then, although he could not see them any longer, he heard them both cry simultaneously:

"Let go! Let go!"

"Jump! Jump!"

"Spread out your wings! And fly! Fly!"

And he did spread them out, like huge white sails with stylish white, red, and blue patterns. Then he jumped and he started flying, flapping his new wings...

The bedroom door swung open abruptly. "Manuel, what for heaven's sake are you doing on the floor?"

"Jesus, I must have fallen from the bed," Manuel said with embarrassment, nursing the side of his head with a hand. "I was having a nightmare."

"I've told you time and time again to stop taking those late afternoon naps," Maria complained sharply. "That's what causes those nightmares! Instead, you should go to bed much earlier at night and stop playing the role of a moth. Night time is for sleeping and day time for working, you know. Not vice-versa."

"I worked on my novel late into the night," he grunted, getting up. "I'm almost done with it."

"What a glorious way to waste your time," she said disgustedly, and slammed the bedroom door shut.

He trudged to the bathroom to pee, glad he had been awakened from the awful nightmare in time by the hard fall and his mother's gruff voice. After he came out of the bathroom, his mother approached him in the kitchen.

"When do you want to have supper?" she asked. "I'm going to the Good Friday services at seven."

"I told you yesterday I was having dinner with Madama Farfalla tonight."

"Oh, that's right," Maria said, brightening up. "Are you going to tell that witch everything you've learned about her?" she said, pressuring him with her eyes.

"Yes," he muttered, regretting having told her what Mrs. Di Giovanni had revealed.

"I always knew there was something evil about her. That's why I always worried about you so much. A mother always has to watch out for her son. She has to be her protector."

Frowning, Manuel started walking away toward his room.

"One more thing: Will you be back in time from that *bruja*'s house to accompany me to the Good Friday services?"

"I don't think so," he said tiredly.

Maria shook her head in critical judgment. "You know, I haven't seen you go to confession or communion in I don't know how long. The past several months, in fact, you've stopped going to church altogether. You send Margarita to Sunday mass alone, and you don't even show up after mass to pick up your girlfriend and walk her home, the poor thing." Maria put her hands on her hips and clucked her tongue in disapproval of her son's actions. "I'm sure it's all those books you've devoured that have turned you against Catholicism. All kinds of silly ideas have gone into your head and done something funny to you up there," she complained. "And now look at you: an unhappy young man tortured by pangs of conscience."

"Are you finished?" Manuel said drily.

He didn't give her the chance to answer and went directly into his room and closed the door.

What a way to upset a son on the last day of his life, Manuel thought sadly. With all her senseless maternal babbling, she had reminded him of some of the very things he didn't want to be reminded of, like Margarita and her possible pregnancy. A few days before, she had called to tell him she had missed her period again, making him more deeply regret his seduction of her the night when her parents had been away on a trip to Union City, New Jersey, an enclave of Cuban immigrants, and he had provided her with a couple of pulverized sleeping pills to be slipped into her chaperoning grandmother's Cuban coffee.

Manuel entered his bedroom and closed the door gently. He went directly to his closet, where several months ago he had put aside the clothes he would wear on this very special day: white pants, white shirt, white socks, white shoes, white everything, except for a blue silk handkerchief he would discreetly tuck into his shirt pocket.

A light tapping came from the door.

"Come in," he said, without turning.

God, it was his mother again. Would she ever stop bugging him?

"While you were sleeping, I went to see attorney Di Fruscia," Maria informed him from his bedroom door. "He's going to demand a personal financial statement and the tax returns for the last three years from your father. He told me half the house your father presently owns can be mine, as well as half of his import-export company. What's more, your father could actually be living, according to Florida law, under the condition of bigamy—which is a crime. That means I could put him in jail if I really wanted to. That's what Mr. Di Fruscia told me. Who knows? Maybe when he gets the letter from my lawyer, he'll think twice about wanting a divorce."

So in reality, Maria didn't want to punish her scandalously cheating husband. All she actually wanted was *to frustrate his intent to obtain a divorce from her.* What a submissive fool! Manolo would probably laugh at her letter as he knew he could play her like a piano any day of the week. On the other hand, the letter Manuel was leaving before he performed his majestic deed would wound his father where the old man would hurt most.

Without acknowledging the presence of his mother, Manuel took the white shirt and pants and laid them on the bed.

"Lately, I get the feeling I could get more of a response

from talking to a wall than to you," Maria snarled, and went away, again shutting the door roughly.

He dressed quickly. It was better to get the ordeal over with as early as possible. He still had the final chapter to write. There was no way he could ask anyone to let this cup pass away from him.

It was a good thing that the letter—his final good-by to his dad and the world—had been penned and typed up. Hopefully, it would be published the following day by the Lawrence *Eagle-Tribune*. The only thing unfinished was the novel, on top of which he would place his scathing farewell note.

In that regard it would be ideal to finish both the novel and his life before midnight—in that order, of course. But it would not be an easy goal to achieve. Somehow he had hit a creative snag, a mental dead-end alley, what was called a writer's block. It was as if a ghostly hand were holding him back from administering the *coup de grâce* to the book and to his existence. The dream he had just had was of no help. In it he had shown the greatest desire to escape imminent death and to live. It definitely was not a good omen as far as he was concerned.

He knew, though, that he could not push himself too hard on this final magnificent project of his, because, if he did, dawn might find him alive, still struggling to write away at his desk to put the finishing touch on the work. By then, however, it would not be Good Friday, and the magical symbolism of the day and the crucial parallelism, clearly underlined in the letter, would have lost their validity.

He climbed the stairs slowly to Madama Farfalla's second-floor apartment, his feet heavy and clumsy as if made of clay. Since the night of the outing in the rain, he had refused to have anything more to do directly with the former diva, asking her by means of a note to put the payment each week for his newspaper-delivery services in an envelope and to slip the envelope under the doormat outside her front door.

It was under these conditions that she had written him a letter which she had slipped into the payday envelope. In her missive she had requested a meeting, a dinner date, which he had postponed numerous times until he had been "good and ready", to use Mrs. Di Giovanni's own terms. And he was indeed now good and ready, not only to sit and eat across the same table with *la Madama*, but also to tear away from her face the mask of deception and hypocrisy she had used to fool him.

When she opened the door, she was the same old Madama Farfalla, all sweetness and quaint charm, except for some striking exterior changes. She was now dressed in something not even remotely close to resembling her old, long black dresses. She had now appeared in a resplendent white kimono replete with embroidered butterflies of all shapes and color combinations.

Her hair also had gone through a metamorphosis. Blacker than ever, it had been raised and set in the form of a thick rising coil held in place with a wide white comb. A couple of large wooden pins and a red rose had been stuck through the hairdo and rode defiantly there.

Her eyes, blacker and shinier than ever, bore elongated eyelashes. A black pencil had outlined the lower rim of each eye. Her cheeks, dabbed with intense rouge, looked more prominent, while her mouth, touched with red lipstick, had attained a strange sort of sensuality, reminding him of a picture of Maria Callas he had seen on the cover of a *Madame Butterfly* album, another gift from Madama

Farfalla. The full-toothed smile made Manuel suspect Farfalla had obtained a set of synthetic teeth. Her new dentures seemed to crown her transformation.

All in all, she gave the impression of being a new person, renewed, rejuvenated, and energized. Like an ancient snake, she had shed her old skin and now sparkled in the new one.

When he failed to return her smile, her face wilted, and she quickly led him in. As he followed her into the dark cavern, the light from the hallway allowed him a good glimpse of the red dragon and black serpent embroidered on the back of her kimono.

"The lasagna is ready," she informed when they reached the kitchen.

She had not forgotten, despite all the time elapsed since his last visit, that lasagna was his favorite Italian dish.

On top of the dinner table, covered with a flaming red tablecloth, stood a gold candelabrum holding three lit candles, the only form of lighting in the room. Suddenly, the bizarre idea hit Manuel that the ambience cast the appearance of some sort of gastronomical High Mass about to be performed inside a home-made catacombs.

Manuel watched the monstrous moving shadow on the wall cast by the candles projecting Madama Farfalla's figure as she brought out a pair of golden goblets and a bottle of Italian wine, a Chianti. From a drawer she produced a corkscrew, which she handed to him.

"Is this *l'ultima volta?*" she suddenly asked in a tremulous voice. "*Lo sento nel mio cuore.*"

She was very perceptive, but not perceptive enough.

"Yes," he said very calmly, as he began to penetrate the bottle's cork with the tip of the screw. Indeed, for just about everything he would do today, he could say it would be the last time ever, *l'ultima volta*.

He remembered the little poem by Jorge Luis Borges called *Límites*, in which the poet talked about a line from Verlaine he would never again remember, a street he would never again walk on, a mirror that had seen him for the last time, a book or a door he had closed until the end of the world.

He thought he now understood perfectly well that little gem of a poem, as perfectly well as he knew this was his Last Supper.

She brought the lasagna and the bread out of the oven.

As she served the food, he noticed her hand trembled. For this reason he poured the wine. Before sitting down, she raised her goblet for a toast, and he rose gallantly to his feet and softly clinked cups with her.

"To our love," she said hoarsely. *"Al nostro amore."*

"To justice," he added, looking at her straight in the eye. *"Alla giustizia."*

With a puzzled, perhaps even frightened, expression on her face, she finally sat down.

"Your teacher, how is he?" she asked when they had began eating. "I hope well."

"I really don't know," Manuel said, looking at his plate and thinking how insipid every type of food, including lasagna, his favorite Italian meal, had become for him as of late. Even the Chianti was not up to par. It had a disagreeable iron taste.

"I do not understand," she said in a small voice.

Manuel took a large swig of wine from his goblet. Then, after wiping his mouth with his red napkin, he said: "Well, Mr. Devlin—and I think that's the teacher whom you're referring to—just plainly dropped out of sight without telling anyone where he was going or why he was leaving the school. There are all kinds of rumors going around, of course, as to what became of him. Some say Devlin was fired by Central Catholic and, because he was death-obsessed, couldn't handle the situation and jumped off a bridge, drowning himself. Others say he flew off to New Orleans to write a book about jazz. Another group says he went off to Brazil on a mission to save the Amazon jungle. Then there is a couple of very imaginative guys who have come with the off-the-wall idea that he was an alien from a distant galaxy and has returned to his 'star people' on his home planet and that that was why he was always talking about 'circles' and 'infinity' and such weird stuff."

Madama Farfalla smiled faintly. "And what do *you* say?" she said, bringing down her goblet.

"I don't really know, as I said," he replied, looking down at his plate again. "And, furthermore, I don't really care," he added through gritted teeth. "Maybe the explanation to his disappearance is the first one I mentioned: He was fired by the Marist brothers for being such an insolent pain in the ass. Only he didn't kill himself because, you see, he doesn't have what it takes. He was just so full of shame and embarrassment he ran with his tail between his legs and didn't say goodbye to anyone."

"You do not like this teacher anymore?"

"No," he grumbled.

"I see," she said very softly, bowing her head.

He drank some more wine, finishing his cup, although he was not fully happy with the bouquet or flavor of the red liquid. When he grasped the bottle to pour himself another cupful, he heard her warn, "You are drinking too much and too fast for your age."

He laughed defiantly. "Wine can do me no harm. It's the blood of the earth, isn't it? Besides, I'm already a man," he said quite seriously, thinking that anyone who could face death as peacefully and fearlessly as he was about to do had to be just that, *a man*—and one with plenty of *cojones*, as Hemingway would have put it. Knowing what he was about to do, he could admire Hemingway now more than ever before. The American writer had done away with his life in 1961, he clearly remembered, just some four months before he, as a ten-year-old boy travelling all alone without either parent, had left Cuba for the United States as part of Operation Peter Pan.

By the time Madama Farfalla and he were through with the main dinner course, Manuel had drunk by himself three-quarters of the Chianti bottle and was feeling a bit tipsy. When she rose and offered him dessert, he ordered Madama Farfalla to sit back down, his voice as stern and harsh as that of a military officer.

"I have something very important to tell you," he informed her.

She did not take her eyes off him as she slowly lowered herself back to her seat.

"For starters, let me just say," he began, pausing to down the small amount of wine left in his goblet and wipe his mouth with the back of a hand, "that as of Saturday I won't be delivering your paper anymore."

Her dark, beautiful long-lashed eyes appeared to squint in sudden pain.

"*Alea jacta est*," he quoted in Latin. "The die is cast. I've crossed my Rubicon and there's no going back. You see, my family and I are moving to an apartment closer to my high school, which my smaller brother will be attending next year, and since I would then have to walk quite a distance to come to deliver your paper, I have asked the *Eagle-Tribune* to find you a new paperboy, that is to say, if you desire to continue receiving the paper."

Madama Farfalla said nothing; she merely puckered her lips as if to hold back a flood of emotions.

"But that's only a small and insignificant part of what I have come to tell you," he went on to say, narrowing his eyes and tightening his grip on his heart. "You see, it just so happens I've found out who you really are," he stated, pausing to observe carefully any further reaction from her, whose face now went completely expressionless and dead, except for a sudden tick in the corner of her painted mouth. "You're not Madama Farfalla. Oh, that may have been your stage name, your artistic name, so to speak. But it's not your real name. Your real name is Floria Giordano, and you are a *whore!*"

Madama Farfalla reeled back against the back of the chair, as if someone had just unloaded a shotgun into her chest, while her hand fluttered over her heart and her mouth dropped open with no sounds being emitted. She stared at him in absolute horror and utter disbelief.

"Calm down," he said in an icy voice. "This is not an opera house. Actually, I want to make this as brief and painless as possible. So let me continue without interruptions of any kind. Do you know a certain woman by the name of Mrs. Di Giovanni?"

She nodded her head, biting her lower lip, a fat tear being squeezed out of each eye.

"She has drawn for me a complete picture of you," he said, straightening up. He was beginning to feel like a judge about to review before the defendant all the incriminating evidence leading to an irrevocable conviction and possible death sentence, in spite of the fact that in the back of his mind also ran the thought he might soon find the tables turned around when he exited this world and entered some other plane of existence, where a Final Judge would stare at him straight in the face.

"The man who lived with you in the apartment below where I now live, who slept with you in the bedroom where I now sleep, was not your husband. He was your lover and you were his mistress. It's Mrs. Di Giovanni who was his real and rightful wife. No, you are not *la Madama Farfalla*. You're simply *la Traviata*, the 'Lady of the Camellias', in short, a tramp, *una puttana!*"

Manuel looked at the silently weeping woman, who had lowered her head in apparent shame, and marveled at the fact that his feelings seemed to be functioning under a cruel protective shield.

"You do not understand the opera," she managed to say through her fitful sobs. "You do not understand *La Traviata*. Violetta Valéry is a good woman! She loves, and she loves *con tutto il suo cuore*. Manuel, *l'amore non è peccato*! *L'amore è la salvezza!*"

Manuel put up a stiff hand. "*Salvezza?* Salvation? And what chance at salvation did you give Mr. Di Giovanni, huh? Because, you see, you're really a combination of Violetta, Turandot, and Lady Macbeth. You're guilty not only of adultery but also of..."

"*Basta!*" she wept, squeezing her hands together in the form of prayer, her makeup beginning to run with the flood of tears and making her look like a sort of crazy Medusa. "*Pietà! Pietà!*"

"Oh, *pietà*. A very fine operatic word. *Pietà*," he repeated with cold sarcasm. "But I'm afraid I'm beyond pity. I'm beyond everything, in fact. I want only to speak the truth at this final hour. So, as I was saying before I was rudely interrupted, you have committed not only adultery but also... *murder*. Yes, *murder*! You're a *murderess*!"

Floria raised her head, the tears flowing freely, wreaking more devastation on her face. "You kill my heart, *il mio cuore*," she said in the thinnest voice. "You destroy my last hope."

"Do I? So now I'm a heart and hope killer. That's a new one," he laughed. "But what about you? You killed your lover in cold blood and probably in his sleep. Plugged two bullets into his old noble head when he was absolutely defenseless. I should know. I have the gun and the unspent bullets."

The once Madama Farfalla, now Floria, gasped, covering her mouth.

"Don't worry. I won't turn you in," he comforted. "I thought you had left the gun for me, but now I see it was just one of your many mistakes. There's no perfect crime, you know. I leave everything to your conscience. I counted the bullets in the cylinder, and there were only four. *Not five*, but *four*. Nobody kills himself with two bullets, you must agree," Manuel said with a Sherlock Holmes smile. "This, my dear lady, corroborates Mrs. Di Giovanni's suspicion that you pulled the trigger and my own theory built on her suspicion that you pulled it twice to make sure the job was done right. Furthermore, according to Mrs. Di Giovanni, the shots went through the victim's left temple. Now the fact is the victim was, Mrs. Di Giovanni tells me, right-handed. And so are you, my dear, I have noticed. One final piece of evidence: a telephone call from the victim to Mrs. Di Giovanni a week or two before his tragic death to tell her he wanted to move in with her at Manor Home, you know, the nursing home where I make paper deliveries. Mrs. Di Giovanni told him she had forgiven him, and then the phone line went dead.

"A few days later your phone was disconnected for good. The following month Mr. Di Giovanni was dead as a result of an apparent suicide.

"But a suicide it wasn't. It was really a homicide, pure and simple, maybe coldly calculated, maybe done in the heat of passion or a rage of jealousy. Who knows? But *murder him you did,*" he said in the rough, thundering voice. "And so now let your conscience, if you actually have one, be the judge of your sin and pronounce the final sentence upon your guilty head."

Floria sunk her face into tremulous hands.

"Most likely you bribed and bought somebody in the police department—you're not as poor as you look; I hear that back in the old country in your heyday you made a bundle at the oldest profession from out of the deep pockets of opera-loving wealthy Italian gentlemen. Maybe you collected on a life insurance policy you secretly bought for Mr. Di Giovanni some years back to overcome the two-year suicide exclusion. You see, I've done all the pertinent research into the case, my dear lady. But one thing is for sure: You can't bribe and buy your own conscience."

Suddenly, Floria raised her head, gripping her chest with one hand, the table with the other.

"Oh, enough with operatic histrionics," Manuel snapped. "You'll find another young paperboy whom you can easily seduce into thinking you're some sort of odd saint, in other words, a blessed Madonna. It worked on me. It almost worked on Rick, the paperboy before me. Mrs. Di Giovanni also told me about how you tried to win his love by bombarding him with gifts and offering to pay for his studies at Central Catholic High School, as you did with me, only you played your cards more cleverly in my case and worked out the secret deal through Sister Helen, who acted as your proxy and in the end turned out to be a traitor.

"Of course, at some point, when it'd have been most convenient for you, you'd have rubbed in my face the fact you had been my benefactor at Central, but I started winning scholarships there and that somewhat upset your plans with me. Rick, however, was, first of all, too dumb and scholastically unprepared to get into Central and, second of all, so extremely insensitive that he was probably never in the least softened by all the tragic stories you fabricated for him about your life, like the one about your poor farmer father, who supposedly committed suicide with the very dagger you have lying on top of your piano after watching a performance of Verdi's *Otello* in Italy. Of course, you called that act *seppuku* to dramatize the situation, as is your custom with everything. But none of this worked on Rick because he was so spiritually thick-skinned. I, on the contrary, proved quite susceptible and gullible to your operatic games and lies."

He cleaned his mouth with the napkin, threw it on the table, and got up to go.

"Please, do not go," she pleaded in an almost inaudible voice. "What you say is not true. What you hear from that woman is a big lie. She is full of hatred and envy. She's like Iago in *Othello*. I explain everything. *Pietà!*"

He started walking away, throwing over his shoulder the words: "I'm finished."

"*Pietà!*" she again sobbed in the most heart-rending way. "I am a good woman. I do things *per amore.*"

Then he did what he knew he should have never done: He turned around and looked at her, his eyes pronouncing the curse and sentence. "There is love that kills," he hissed through his contorted mouth and fiery eyes.

She slowly extended an arm, the arm whose hand had, seconds before, been clutching at her left breast.

Slowly he walked back to her, his heart frozen still, his mind fully numb, and laid the softest kiss on her wet cheek.

She then tried to grab him by the shirt, as though her life depended on it, but she was no match for him and he easily managed to push her away, almost making her fall.

He sauntered away quickly.

"*Addio!*" she cried.

"*Addio.* I must carry out what remains to be done," he said to the darkness of the parlor, where he knew stood the cobweb-assaulted piano, on top of whose dusty console ominously rested the old dagger.

Chapter Xx

*O*h, child, how can you hope to hear the sounds of one hand clapping above that hellish cacophony coming from the first part of that Liszt symphony? Have you forgotten my lesson that every coin, although having two sides, is still one coin, that every playing record, although having two faces, is still just one record, that every clapping, although the product of two hands, is still the clapping of one?

I have returned from the stars, oh clumsy apprentice, to remind you of that lesson, to turn back the flood you have started but cannot end, to put the final touches on your unfinished work.

From your bed, curled into rising spirals of time and compassion, I watch you attentively and lovingly. For I have come to protect and save you, I who have already been nailed twice for you, once to the Tree of Death and then to the Tree of Life, and twice to the one and same tree under the sun and moon.

You lie with your head on the notebook filled with your soul's outpourings, the right hand still clutching the black revolver on the desk. Once you came very close to leaping over the edge, but I held you back, putting preventive thoughts and images in your head. You saw yourself, a Peter Pan boy, in a Pan Am four-propeller airplane in Havana's International Airport. You were ten years old and on your way to unknown lands with Nordic people with different customs and a strange language. You gazed through the airplane window and suddenly spotted your family, your father and your mother and your younger brother, waving good-by to you with handkerchiefs from the roof top of the airport building. And your heart wanted to burst with sadness.

The memories made your eyes well up with tears, and you put the gun down once more.

I did not make my move then because, wise sorcerer that I am, I knew well the time was not ripe. But things now are rushing to a point and a center, and so I must shed the skin of inertia and begin to work my way toward you. I slide off the bed and writhe along the floor toward the desk chair and clamber up your leg and thigh.

You stir, not because of me, whom you do not yet feel, but because of her, whose lugubrious piano-playing of Verdi's *Requiem* has abruptly stopped and ceased competing with your Liszt. A short while later, the pattering of her feet is heard coming directly from above your room. Soon other musical sounds float downward, sounds you recognize as those from the last act of a Puccini opera.

However, it does not even remotely occur to you that at that very moment *un sacrificio* is in the making to ease the rebirth.

You turn your head as I begin to twist up your torso.

When I reach your head, I momentarily cover it with my hood. You see the first rays of the new dawn burst through your bedroom window, like knife stabs, and you shake your head, deeply disappointed.

Then, knowing there is now no time to lose as the moment of truth draws near, I break into your mouth, squirming into your being until I reach the fourth chakra, at the level of the heart, where I breathe your air and you mine.

At last you rise and approach your record player. You lift Liszt's *Dante Symphony* record and turn it onto its other side, the side that reads *Purgatorio* and *Magnificat*.

Before going back to your desk, you look up and wonder why on earth she is playing on her phonograph the last act of *Madame Butterfly*, particularly at such a desolate hour of the morning. Puzzled, you go sit back at your desk, but not before picking up the revolver from your desk and placing the gun on your bed.

Suddenly, you jump to your feet, terrified by a thought.

When you look up again, it is too late.

Il sacrificio has been consummated.

You hear the heavy, hard thud followed by the small, sharp metallic one.

You stare upward, skyward, frozen to the floor.

Then you see the thousand white petals breaking through the ceiling into your room, turning into exquisitely fine butterflies, white, red, and blue. And breathing them into your lungs and mine, you scream at the top of your lungs as you look up at the ceiling: "Farfalla! Farfalla! Farfalla! Please don't go!"

He turned to his left as he heard his bedroom door open.

His mother stood in the door frame, holding something in her hand. Her face looked expressionless.

"I already called the police," she informed him. "It was all I could do. Her front door is shut."

"She's dead," Manuel said in a cracked voice.

"I never imagined this would happen," Maria said softly.

"It's my fault."

Pietà, pietà, pietà echoed in his conscience like a hammer.

"No, it's not," she argued. "If it's anybody's fault, it's mine. I was very rough on you," she admitted in a quaking voice, "and in return maybe you were rough on her. I think I was jealous of her and pushed you to do and say things you really didn't want to. It was very stupid of me. Suffering has made me stupid." She pressed her lips together hard. "I should have never made you suffer for my suffering." Then her eyes locked on the revolver lying on Manuel's bed and she gave a gasp. She stiffened. "Give me the gun," she said firmly.

Manuel did not hesitate and handed her the revolver. At that precise moment he remembered the shootout.

How could he have been so foolish as to have become obsessed with throwing away his life when he had fought so hard to win on that basketball court on some remote Andover park? He had wanted to live so much then! How could things have changed so fast?

He then recalled the dead woman's last pronouncement: *"L'amore è la salvezza!"*

He looked at his mom straight in the eyes, for the first time in months or perhaps in years.

And he saw the crow's feet around her hazel eyes.

Oh, my God, he thought, feeling his heart tremble, my

mother is growing old and, up to this moment, I hadn't noticed. One day she, too, will die.

"We don't want a double tragedy in our hands," she sighed. "I'll give the gun to the police. They'll know what to do with it. I'll tell them I found it in the trash tank outside."

Manuel nodded in agreement.

"This is for you," she now said, and held out, with the hand not holding the firearm, an object that looked like a small thin booklet. "It's a bank deposit book in your name. All the money in it was put there by Madama Farfalla. She said it was for your college education or anything else you might need the money for. I never imagined she was that wealthy. She gave me this when I returned from the Good Friday services. She also told me she was going far away. Obviously, I misunderstood the meaning of this. Otherwise, I would have done something about it, believe me."

The son offered the mother a shy grateful smile.

Manuel and Maria looked at each other for the longest time. Then, after placing the gun on top of the chest of drawers by the door, she began to make her way toward him with hesitant small steps.

He was the first to open his arms, and she immediately embraced him, as if for the first time in a lifetime.

When he heard the approaching din of the police sirens and felt the wetness of his mother's tears on his shoulder, he hugged her more tightly.